PROFESSOR

GARGOYLE

PROFESSOR

GARGOYLE

TALES FROM
LOVECRAFT
MIDDLE SCHOOL #1

By
CHARLES GILMAN

Illustrations by
EUGENE SMITH

QUIRK BOOKS
PHILADELPHIA

Library of Congress Cataloging in Publication Number: 2011946052

ISBN: 978-1-59474-591-1
Printed in China
Typeset in Bembo, House Monster Fonts, and Melior

Designed by Doogie Horner
Cover photography by Jonathan Pushnik
Cover model: Frank Baker
Illustrations by Eugene Smith
Cover lenticular by National Graphics, Inc.
Production management by John J. McGurk

Quirk Books
215 Church Street
Philadelphia, PA 19106
quirkbooks.com

10 9 8 7 6 5 4 3 2

This book
is for Sam

CHAPTER ONE

Robert Arthur was surrounded by strangers.

He stood outside the entrance to Lovecraft Middle School, watching the students pass by, searching for a familiar face. Everybody was talking to someone. Kids were joking and laughing and goofing around. But Robert didn't recognize a single person.

Earlier that summer, his neighborhood had been redistricted. This was a fancy way of saying that all of his old friends were attending Franklin Middle School, in the north part of town, but somehow Robert got stuck attending Lovecraft Middle School, in the south part of town.

His mother told him there was no say in the matter;

it was just the luck of the draw.

"But you're going to love it," she promised. "They spent millions of dollars building this school. It's brand-new. State of the art. With a swimming pool and digital chalkboards and everything. It's such an incredible opportunity!"

Robert wasn't so sure. He would have happily traded the swimming pool and digital chalkboards for the chance to be with his old friends. He had a hundred different worries: *Who would sit with him at lunch? What if he needed help opening his locker? Wasn't anybody from his old school here?*

Beside the main entrance of the school was a large digital billboard with an animated message:

WELCOME, STUDENTS!
PLEASE REPORT TO THE ATHLETIC ARENA
FOR THE RIBBON-CUTTING CEREMONY!

It might have been faster to walk through the building, but Robert wasn't in a hurry. He took his time, circling the outside of the school, marveling at how quickly it seemed to have sprung from the earth.

Six months earlier, this was all abandoned farmland, full of weeds and mud puddles and sticker bushes. Now there was a four-story classroom building, tennis courts, a baseball diamond, and lush green grass as far as the eye could see.

When Robert reached the athletic stadium, the bleachers were packed with spectators: students, teachers, parents, news reporters—everyone in town had come to witness the ribbon-cutting ceremony. Everyone except Robert's mother, a nurse, who worked the early shift at Dunwich Memorial Hospital. Most mornings she was out the door before Robert woke up, so she rarely attended school presentations or class trips. Sometimes this bothered Robert, but today he was grateful. He knew the only thing more embarrassing than sitting alone at his new middle school would be sitting with his mommy. All the other kids were sitting with their friends.

Robert climbed halfway up the bleachers and

squeezed between two clusters of giggling girls. He tried smiling at them.

None of the girls smiled back.

The ribbon-cutting ceremony was already under way. First the mayor thanked the governor. Then the governor stood up and thanked the teachers' union. Then a bunch of teachers got up and thanked the parents' association. Then a bunch of parents cheered and thanked Principal Slater.

Finally Principal Slater stood up with oversized scissors and sliced the long green ribbon in half. At precisely that moment, the clouds turned gray and a low drum of thunder rolled across the sky.

It was weird, Robert thought. Just one minute ago, it had been a perfectly pleasant and sunny day. Now, suddenly, it looked like rain.

Fortunately, the ceremony was almost over. The grand finale was a special performance by the Dunwich High School marching band, complete with drums, brass, and color guard. They paraded across the field playing "The Stars and Stripes Forever."

Robert glanced over his shoulder, peering up at the bleachers, scanning the faces. There must have been four hundred kids in the arena. He knew that, sooner or later, he'd have to recognize someone.

And then he did.

The worst possible someone.

Oh, no.

Robert immediately faced forward.

But it was too late. He'd been spotted.

"Hey, Robert! Is that you? Robert Arthur?"

He couldn't believe his rotten luck. *Glenn Torkells?* The one person he knew at Lovecraft Middle School—and it was *Glenn Torkells?* The bully who had tormented him for years?

"Robert! I'm talking to you!"

Definitely Glenn Torkells.

Robert tried ignoring him. His mother used to tell him to ignore the bullies and eventually they would leave him alone. *Yeah, right.*

"I know that's you, Robert. I got a real good memory and I never forget a face." Something slimy hit the back of Robert's neck. He reached up and peeled it off: a half-chewed gummy worm.

"Turn around and look at me."

Robert knew that Glenn would get what he wanted, sooner or later. Glenn always did. Robert turned around and another gummy worm struck him right in the forehead.

Glenn laughed uproariously. "Haw-haw! Bull's-eye!"

He was seated two rows behind Robert, looking much like he did back in elementary school—only bigger. He wore the same green army jacket and the same grubby blue jeans. His dark blond hair was still plastered to his forehead, still looking like he'd cut it himself with dull scissors. Glenn had always been the biggest kid in the class, but over the summer he'd ballooned into the Incredible Hulk.

"What do you want?" Robert asked.

Glenn popped a gummy worm into his mouth and began working his jaw. "Dweeb tax," he said. "Pay up."

Robert sighed. Glenn had been collecting the

dweeb tax for part of fifth grade and all of sixth. It was a one-dollar penalty he imposed on Robert for various "infractions"—tripping or stammering or wearing ugly pants or other "crimes" that Glenn dreamed up.

Robert glanced around, hoping to spot a teacher who might intervene. That never happened at his last school, but he thought maybe Lovecraft Middle School would be different.

No such luck. Everyone was watching the marching band on the field. The girls on either side of Robert were chattering among themselves.

"Hurry up, Nerdbert," Glenn said. "You think you're the only kid in this school who owes me?"

Earlier that morning, Robert's mother had given him an extra five dollars of spending money, to celebrate his first day as a middle school student.

Robert retrieved one of those dollars and passed it to Glenn. His tormentor shook his head and smiled, revealing flecks of chewed-up gummy worm in his teeth.

"It's gonna be *two* dollars here in middle school," Glenn explained. "We're not little kids anymore."

CHAPTER TWO

After the marching band had finished playing, Principal Slater directed the students to find their lockers and then proceed to their homerooms.

As the bleachers emptied, Robert moved nimbly through the crowd, careful to stay several steps ahead of Glenn Torkells.

He noticed a girl hurrying alongside him.

Looking at him.

She was short and skinny, dressed in a white T-shirt and blue jeans and carrying a beat-up skateboard. She had dark brown hair that fell past her shoulders and wore a dozen jangling bracelets on her wrists. She smiled, revealing a mouthful of metal braces.

"You've got worms in your hair," she said.

"Excuse me?"

"Gummy worms. In your scalp."

Robert reached up and shook them loose. "Thanks."

"You're gonna have to stand up to him."

"Stand up to who?"

"You know who."

Robert flushed. Was there anything more embarrassing than getting advice on bullies from a cute girl?

"Glenn and I are friends," Robert quickly explained. "That's just a stupid game we play. I owed him two dollars from the other night."

"He called it a dweeb tax."

"See, that's part of the game."

The girl wasn't buying it, Robert could tell.

"I'm Karina," she said. "Karina Ortiz."

"Robert Arthur."

"I know," she said. "I heard him taunting you."

"He wasn't taunting me."

"Friends don't throw chewed–up gummy worms in

your hair," she said. "I was there. I watched the whole thing."

"Well, maybe next time you should mind your own business."

The words came out louder than Robert intended. Karina raised both hands in a defensive gesture, like he'd just come at her with his fists. "Hey, suit yourself," she said. "You just looked like you needed a friend, that's all."

Karina dropped her skateboard to the asphalt, pushed off with one foot, and quickly zoomed away from him, swerving around the other students with remarkable balance and precision.

Almost immediately, Robert wished he could apologize and somehow take the words back. But it was too late. Karina was the first friendly person to approach him at Lovecraft Middle School, and he'd managed to scare her away.

He followed the crowd of students up the stairs and into the central corridor of the school, a frenzy of color and sound and energy.

Instead of bulletin boards, the hallways of Lovecraft

Middle School featured large high-definition LCD screens with animated announcements of soccer try-outs and chorus practice. Sleek metal lockers lined the walls; instead of old-fashioned combination dials, they had ten-button digital touch pads. Up and down the hallway, kids were lining up to stow their backpacks and lunches.

Robert walked to his locker—A119—and entered the passcode he'd received in the mail. Each button made a satisfying chirp when he pressed it, and then the locker door opened with a gentle pneumatic *whooooosh*.

In the distance, Robert heard a girl shriek, but he thought nothing of it. Girls in sixth and seventh grade were always shrieking about something or another.

His new locker was divided by a metal shelf into two sections. There was a tall bottom section with a hook where he could hang his coat and a short top section, near the air vents, where he could store his brown-bag lunch.

Robert studied the top section and blinked.

Perched on the shelf, twitching its nose, was a large white rat.

Elsewhere in the hallway, another girl screamed. Then another, and another. A teacher yelled, "Get back!" and Robert felt something brush past his legs. He stumbled away from the locker as the white rat sprang toward him, landing on his chest and leapfrogging over his shoulder.

"Get it off me!" someone shouted.

"There's another one!"

"It's in my hair!"

More rats brushed past his feet—there were dozens now, darting under sneakers, gnashing their teeth, squealing and snarling and stampeding down the hall.

Up until this moment, Robert's life had been fairly quiet and ordinary. He had the same interests and hobbies as a million other twelve-year-old boys. He spent his days in school; he spent his nights doing homework and messing around on the computer. He'd never experienced anything that might have prepared him for a swarm of wild rats.

Yet while the rest of his classmates were freaking out, Robert remained calm.

He understood he had just two choices: He could scream and panic like the rest of his classmates. Or he could sit tight for a few moments and hope the rats would charge toward the nearest exit.

Which is exactly what happened. The stampede reached the open doors at the end of the hallway and fanned out across the lush green lawns surrounding the school. The students watched after them, awestruck.

"I don't believe it," said the boy standing next to Robert. "They spend a trillion dollars building this place and it's already full of rats? How's that possible?"

Good question, Robert thought.

He knelt to study the inside of his locker. The metal walls and floors were intact; there were no gaps or cracks or holes. There were no places where a rat might have squeezed its way into his locker.

Robert knew middle school would be strange, but this was ridiculous.

CHAPTER

THREE

Incredibly, the strangest part of Robert's first day at Lovecraft Middle School was yet to come.

Most of his teachers were very nice. His American History teacher promised a class trip to Philadelphia, where students would tour the National Constitution Center. His Mathematics teacher demonstrated a neat trick for adding large numbers without a calculator or even a pencil. And all of his teachers boasted about the school's extraordinary new facilities. They claimed Lovecraft Middle School was the most environmentally responsible school on the East Coast; much of the building was constructed from recycled materials. They seemed like good teachers who were proud to be working in a good school.

Then Robert went to Science.

As soon as he arrived, he noticed Glenn Torkells seated on the far side of the classroom. Robert ducked his head and grabbed a desk near the door.

There was no sign of a teacher, but the students had plenty to admire while they waited: chemistry flasks and beakers and enough test tubes to stock a mad scientist's laboratory. At the front of the classroom was a life-size model of a human skeleton. In the back were a dozen aquariums housing tropical fish, lizards, a hamster, and other small animals.

The seventh-period bell rang and still no teacher arrived. Robert's classmates continued to chat away, but the mood had changed. Something was wrong.

He checked his class schedule.

PERIOD 7 – SCIENCE
MRS. KINSKI – ROOM 213

He was in the correct room at the correct time.

But where was Mrs. Kinski?

The girl on Robert's left turned to him. "I think you should go to the principal's office," she said. "Tell them we're waiting for a teacher."

"Me?" Robert asked.

"Don't listen to her," said the girl sitting on his right. "She likes to boss people around."

"I do not."

"Do too."

Robert looked from left to right and back again. Both girls had fair skin and long red hair. They looked so similar, they could have been sisters.

In fact, they looked virtually identical.

"Wait a second," he said. "Are you two—"

"Twins," they said simultaneously, almost sighing, as if they were tired of answering the question.

"Cool," he said, because he couldn't think of anything else to say. "I'm Robert."

The girls didn't bother to introduce themselves.

Suddenly the door to the classroom swung open and Robert looked up, expecting to see Mrs. Kinski.

Instead there was an old man, tall and gnarled and dressed in a jacket and tie. He seemed surprised to find the classroom full of students. His cold blue eyes surveyed the desks, taking everything in. He did not blink.

"Good afternoon," he finally said. His voice was rich and deep and smooth as polished wood. "I hope you'll forgive my tardiness."

He lumbered toward the front of the classroom and laid a worn leather satchel on his desk. Without a word, he turned to the blackboard, picked up a piece of chalk, and began scratching some notes:

> *Rattus norvegicus*
> Kingdom: Animalia
> Phylum: Chordata
> Class: Mammalia
> Order: Rodentia

Robert watched in astonishment with the rest of his class. "Excuse me?"

The teacher whirled around. "Yes, young man?"

Robert immediately regretted opening his mouth, but someone had to ask the obvious question. "What about Mrs. Kinski?"

"Kinski?" The teacher scrutinized Robert through his bushy eyebrows. "Kinski, Kinski. Why does that name sound familiar?"

Robert held up his class schedule. "It says she's teaching seventh-period science. Here. In Room 213."

"You mean the substitute! Of course! Mrs. Kinski is one of our many wonderful substitute instructors. She'd been assigned to cover my duties while I was, ah, recovering. From illness. But as you can see I'm feeling perfectly fine, so her services are no longer required. I am Professor Garfield Goyle and *I* will be your seventh-grade science teacher."

Robert had seen some kooky teachers over the years, but this guy was far and away the strangest. Professor Goyle didn't even bother to take attendance. He just turned back to the chalkboard and began sketching an anatomical drawing of a rat skeleton. It was extremely detailed and took him the better part of ten minutes. He drew forcefully and furiously, and several times the chalk snapped in his grip.

When the drawing was finally complete, he labeled the bones one at a time—the sternum, the scapula, the tibia, the thoracic vertebrae . . .

One of the twins raised her hand.

"Excuse me, Mr. Goyle?"

He didn't turn around. "*Professor* Goyle."

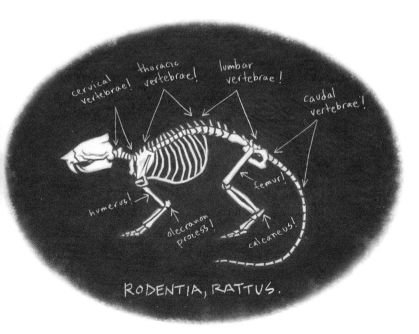

"Professor Goyle, is this going to be on the test?"

"I don't understand the question." He went right on labeling the head of the rodent: the incisors and the mandible and the maxilla.

"I mean, should we be taking notes or something?"

Again, the chalk snapped in Goyle's fingers; the broken pieces clattered to the floor.

He turned around to face the class, looking weary from all the frenzied scribbling.

"I understand," he said, "that many of you were disturbed by this morning's incident. This is completely understandable. Humankind has long associated rats with disease and filth. In fourteenth-century Europe, rats carried the dreaded black death, a plague that killed some one hundred million people." Professor Goyle laughed. "Can you imagine that, children? A hundred million humans? Wiped off the earth by a bunch of tiny rodents? They're truly deadly creatures! Much more dangerous than they appear!"

The class stared back at him. If he was trying to put them at ease, he wasn't doing a very good job.

Goyle walked over to the window and glanced outside. "You need to remember that, six months ago, all of this property was farmland. Trees. Streams. Hundreds of natural ecosystems invisible to the naked eye. The rats were probably quite happy living here. They had food, water, shelter, everything they needed." His expression darkened. "Until man came along and bulldozed all their underground burrows. Destroying their homes in the blink of an eye. Now what would you have these creatures do? They needed a new place to hide, and the result was this morning's unfortunate surprise."

The other students were nodding as if this made perfect sense, but Robert wasn't satisfied at all. It didn't explain how a rat ended up *inside* his locker. But Robert was too shy to ask another question, so he didn't raise his hand. He figured it was no big deal. If everyone else in class accepted Goyle's explanation, then it was probably—

"Uh, Professor Goyle?" Glenn asked. His voice was full of uncertainty; Robert couldn't remember the last time he'd heard Glenn ask a question in class. "I hear what you're saying, but I found one of those rats *inside* my locker. It was there, like, *before* I opened it."

Professor Goyle nodded. "An adult rat can gnaw through bone, brick, concrete, even lead piping. Your school lockers are made from sixteen-gauge sheet metal, a much thinner material. No match for the teeth of a rodent."

"Yeah, but I checked my locker," Glenn continued. "There weren't any holes in it."

Now Goyle seemed irritated.

"What's your name, young man?"

"Uh, Glenn?"

"Glenn what? Do you have a family name?"

"Glenn Torkells."

"Mr. Torkells, are you sure there were no holes in your locker? You're absolutely sure?"

"Yeah, I checked all over. No holes. Just the air vents in the door."

"Just the air vents in the door!" Goyle exclaimed. "Now we're getting somewhere! Tell me, Mr. Torkells, how would you describe the width of those vents? Did you happen to notice?"

"Maybe half an inch?"

"Maybe half an inch," Goyle said, smiling now. "And did you know, Mr. Torkells, that the rat is the only known mammal that can literally collapse its own skeleton at will, allowing it to squeeze through spaces as narrow as half an inch?"

"I did not know that," Glenn mumbled, and the whole classroom laughed.

"Of course you didn't! Because you're too busy wasting my time with stupid questions!"

Robert gasped. It was the first time he'd ever heard a teacher describe any question as "stupid."

"May I suggest," Goyle continued, "that you listen obediently to my lecture, like the rest of your peers? Then maybe you'll learn something. Do you think you can manage that?"

Glenn nodded, face flushed, and slouched down sheepishly into his chair. Professor Goyle returned to the chalkboard and continued labeling the rat.

Robert couldn't believe it. For just one moment—for the tiniest split second—*he actually felt sorry for Glenn Torkells.*

It was by far the strangest thing that happened to Robert all day.

CHAPTER

FOUR

When Robert came home from school, his mother wanted to hear all about his first day at Lovecraft Middle School. Mrs. Arthur felt terrible about missing the ribbon-cutting ceremony, and she asked Robert to describe all the details. He told her about the mayor and the governor and the marching band. He didn't mention Glenn or the gummy worms.

"Oh, it sounds wonderful!" Mrs. Arthur exclaimed. "Absolutely wonderful!" She sat across from Robert at the kitchen table and placed a bowl of carrot sticks between them. "We deserve this, Robert. Do you know what I mean?"

"Sure," he said.

"I know these last few years have been tough for you. I'm out the door at six thirty every morning. I can't make you a hot breakfast. I can't go on school trips. It's been hard." She reached across the table and held his hand. "But this is a real turning point. You're a smart kid in a great school. If you study and work hard, everything's going to turn out fine."

Robert couldn't remember the last time he'd seen his mother so happy. He decided not to mention the rats, at least not right now. There was no point in spoiling the moment.

For the next few days, everything at Lovecraft was perfectly normal. There were no more rodents in the lockers and Robert's class schedule kept him away from Glenn for most of the day. At lunchtime, he ate by himself, but that was okay; he always brought a book to read so it would appear as if he'd purposefully chosen to sit alone.

Robert loved all kinds of books, especially horror, science fiction, and fantasy. His favorite stories were about kids with strange and magical powers—kids who were wizards or werewolves or cyborgs. Robert often daydreamed that he would one day discover his own supernatural powers and then he wouldn't be quite so normal. In the meantime, he went to the public library every week and came home with stacks of books.

He'd heard that Lovecraft had an enormous library, but he didn't see it firsthand until the second week of school. His English teacher, Mr. Loomis, told the students to grab their backpacks. "You're in for a real treat today," he promised them. "We're going to see one of the finest school libraries in the entire state."

"Finally," Robert mumbled to himself.

Mr. Loomis must have overheard him, because he winked. "I'm excited, too," he said. "Wait until you see this place."

The Lovecraft Middle School library was nearly as big as the gymnasium. A steel-and-glass ceiling arched grandly overhead, filling the room with a warm natural light. Huge bookshelves twisted along the perimeter like the walls of a labyrinth; it would be easy to get lost in them for hours at a time, Robert thought. Standing among the books were life-size statues of famous authors: Mark Twain, Edgar Allan Poe, Mary Shelley, Louisa May Alcott . . .

"Over here, Robert!" Mr. Loomis called. "Stay with the class, all right?"

The other students had already settled in the media center. It was a room within a room, set apart by giant Plexiglass walls that looked out over the rest of the library. Inside were computers, listening stations, and a rack full of handheld e-readers.

An elderly woman with cat-eye glasses was demonstrating for the students how to use the e-readers. "These can be filled with downloaded books and checked out from the library—as long as you're very careful with them, of course. Personally, I'm a little old-fashioned. I still prefer the feel of a real book with real pages. The best feeling in the world, if you ask me. But we have to embrace the future, don't we, children?"

Mr. Loomis cleared his throat. "Class, allow me to introduce Ms. Lavinia. She's the head librarian."

Ms. Lavinia put down the e-reader and walked around the media center, handing each student a full-color map on glossy paper, with all the different sections of the library labeled: biography, history, science fiction, mystery, and so on. "We'll spend today learning how to find library books and borrow them. You'll see I've written the name of a different book on every map. To complete the assignment, you need to find your book and borrow it from the library. You're allowed to help your classmates, so let's work together, all right?"

Robert looked at the top of his map. His title was:

THE ADVENTURES OF FANGS DUNGAREE,
TEENAGE VAMPIRE COWBOY DETECTIVE
#1: THE CASE OF THE FLAMING HORSESHOE
By M. J. Hetter
Section: General Fiction – Mystery – Paranormal

Robert raised his hand. "Could I get a different book?"

"I'm sorry," Ms. Lavinia said, "there's only one per student."

Robert couldn't believe his rotten luck. He liked books about kids with supernatural powers, but this was ridiculous. *The Adventures of Fangs Dungaree* sounded like the dumbest book in the world.

"If you don't like your selection," Ms. Lavinia continued, "you're welcome to choose more than one title. Students may borrow up to five books at any time."

The other students seemed happy with their assignments and everyone quickly spread out across the library. Robert decided he would find *Fangs Dungaree* first and then use the rest of his time to find books that he would actually enjoy.

Using the map as a guide, Robert plunged into a maze of shelves labeled GENERAL FICTION, and the chatter of his classmates faded behind him. After three left turns and two right turns he arrived in GENERAL FICTION – MYSTERY and a few steps later found himself in GENERAL FICTION – MYSTERY – PARANORMAL.

When he finally looked up again, the shelves

seemed to have grown taller. It must have been a trick of the light—the tops of the shelves appeared to be leaning over him ever so slightly, like trees blocking out the sun.

Tracing the spines of the books with his finger, he followed the alphabet along its erratic path, from *A* to *B* to *C* to *D*. The route was slow going and full of unexpected twists and turns; the library had many more books than he'd realized.

By the time Robert arrived in the *H* section, he felt like he had walked the length of a football field. He found all seventeen *Fangs Dungaree* mysteries by M. J. Hetter, grabbed *The Case of the Flaming Horseshoe*, and stuffed it in his backpack. Then he turned to leave but realized he couldn't remember which direction he'd come from.

It was weird. He'd meant to follow the alphabet backward—*H* to *G* to *F* to *E*, until he was back where he started—but somehow he'd taken a wrong turn. The surrounding books were wholly unfamiliar. Robert turned left and right and left again. Books blurred past him; all the corridors looked the same. He consulted the map but couldn't orient himself; somehow, he'd managed to get completely lost.

When Robert looked up again, he saw a flash of movement—a girl in a white T-shirt, darting around a corner.

"Hello?" Robert called.

She didn't stop or turn around. Robert followed her.

"Excuse me? Hello?"

The girl moved faster, slipping around another corner, just out of sight. Robert began to run, heading deeper and deeper into the seemingly endless corridors.

From out of nowhere, he sensed a pungent odor of moldy mothballs. The smell seemed out of character for Lovecraft Middle School, where everything was sparkling and polished and brand-new.

"Wait up!" Robert called.

He followed the girl around a corner and found himself facing a dead end.

The girl was gone.

"Hello?"

No answer. No footsteps. Nothing but silence.

Robert walked all the way to the very end of the corridor. In the shadows between two of the bookshelves was a tall, narrow doorway—so narrow he would have to turn sideways to squeeze through. It was bordered with dark brown wood and etched with all kinds of mysterious symbols, like the random characters that would pop up on his computer screen whenever it decided to crash.

Robert felt a chill. The smell of moldy mothballs was strongest right here. His heart pounding, he took a deep breath, grabbed the straps of his backpack, and plunged into the shadows.

CHAPTER
FIVE

All he'd done was step through the narrow doorway from one section of the library into another. But Robert felt like he'd somehow switched speeds—as if he'd stepped from a moving escalator onto steady ground. He nearly stumbled over his own feet.

In front of him was a long, rickety staircase. As he climbed it, the wooden boards creaked and groaned beneath his feet; the handrails were covered with a fine layer of dust. At the top of the stairs was a patchwork curtain made from dozens of fabric scraps. Robert stepped around it and found himself in what appeared to be a large, dusty attic.

Quilts and blankets were tied to the rafters to keep out the drafts, but they weren't helping much; the room was extremely cold. Here and there were a dozen mismatched bookshelves, seemingly placed at random. The books themselves had leather bindings and yellowed pages. Everything was covered in dark wood and steeped in long shadows.

Even stranger, the room had no windows, no fire exits, and none of the digital gadgetry found throughout Lovecraft Middle School. The attic was straight out of the nineteenth century.

Robert approached a round wooden table in the center of the room. On its surface was an open book, facedown. Robert shuddered. The book's spine appeared to be an actual spine—the bright white vertebrae of what might be a snake or lizard.

There was no title on the cover. Inside were words Robert had never seen before. One chapter was called *Gnopf-Keh*. Another was called *Gyaa-Yothn*. The pages were filled with outlandish black-and-white illustrations of strange beasts, flaming skulls, and volcanic landscapes.

"Freaky," he whispered, unzipping his backpack and placing the book inside it.

"If you're looking for normal," a voice said, "you've come to the wrong place."

Robert whirled around and there was Karina Ortiz, dressed in a white T-shirt and blue jeans.

"What is this place?"

"It's an attic," she shrugged. "Pretty cool hangout, don't you think?"

Robert studied the floor plan he'd received from Ms. Lavinia. There were sections of the library labeled NONFICTION and MEDIA ROOM but he didn't see anything indicating an attic.

"The map's useless, Robert."

"That's why I called to you for help. I'm lost."

She smiled, flashing her braces. "You *were* lost. Now you're with me. I know exactly where we are." She patted the space on the floor beside her. "Why don't you hang out for a little bit?"

"I'm in the middle of English class," he reminded her. "I'm supposed to be looking for books."

"Is that kid Glenn still bothering you?"

Robert felt another flush of shame. "You know, I'm sorry I snapped at you the other day. But I really don't like to talk about Glenn."

"You need to stand up to him. I know you're scared of him. But the best way to deal with your fears is to face them head-on."

This sounded like terrible advice to Robert. He knew that if he faced Glenn head-on, he'd end up with his head shoved into a toilet.

"Tell me something," he said. "What are *you* afraid of?"

"Spiders."

"No, I mean your *worst* fear. What's the thing you dread more than anything else?"

"Seriously, it's spiders," Karina said. "I hate everything about them. The hairy legs, the twitchy bodies, the silk squirting out of their butts. They're disgusting."

Robert looked around the room. "Then maybe you should find a different place to hang out. This attic looks like it's full of them."

Karina shook her head. "Nobody bothers me here. It's pretty hard to find. You're welcome to stay as long as you want. I've got all kinds of cool stuff."

The attic was full of things that a person might not expect to find in a school library: a dressmaker's dummy, a half-strung cello, a battered aluminum rowboat. But the strangest of these was a large wooden door at the far end of the room. It was barricaded with three thick wooden planks. They were arranged haphazardly, as if they'd been nailed in a hurry.

"What's that?" he asked.

"Emergency exit."

It didn't look like any emergency exit that Robert had seen before. "Why is it nailed shut?"

"You're only supposed to open it in an emergency."

Robert wasn't sure he believed her, but he didn't have time to ask a lot of questions.

"I better go," he said. "Can you draw me a map or something?"

Karina smiled. "You won't have any trouble getting back, Robert. I promise. Just walk down the stairs

and you'll find your way."

Robert didn't believe her, but he wasn't going to stick around and argue. Something about the attic felt weird; it seemed like a forbidden place, and he worried they'd get in trouble if a teacher caught them messing around in it.

He zipped his backpack closed and slung it over his shoulders. It was much heavier now with the old book inside.

"And Robert?" Karina called.

He stopped. "Yeah?"

"I don't know a lot of people here. So if you ever want to hang out, just come back to this room, all right?"

Robert stepped around the curtain. He descended the rickety wooden staircase and squeezed through the narrow doorway. Once again he felt the same tingling sensation—and, this time, the floor seemed to speed up beneath him, yanking him forward.

CHAPTER SIX

Somehow Karina was right: It took only a minute of wandering through the shelves before Robert turned a corner and ran right into his English teacher.

"There you are!" Mr. Loomis exclaimed. "I've spent half the class looking for you."

"I'm sorry. I was lost."

His teacher grinned. "I know the feeling. A library this good, I could get lost for days."

Robert liked Mr. Loomis. He wore pastel-colored sweater vests, loved books, and never needed to raise his voice. And he didn't insist on being called "Professor" like a certain crazy science teacher.

"Did you find anything good?" Mr. Loomis asked.

Robert patted his backpack. "Right here."

"You'll need to check them out before you leave," Mr. Loomis said. "There are lending kiosks near the entrance. Key in your student ID and the touch screen will guide you the rest of the way. Hurry now, Robert, before the bell rings."

Robert walked over to the lending kiosks, which looked like the self-checkout machines in supermarkets. He unzipped his backpack, reached inside for the books, and felt a sudden shooting pain in his hand.

Something was biting him.

He dropped the backpack and the pain stopped. He looked down at his palm. There were two red marks on his thumb. Not deep enough to be punctures. But almost definitely teeth marks.

Teeth marks?

He glanced around the library. None of the kids were watching him. And Mr. Loomis was over by the media center, chatting with Ms. Lavinia.

Robert zipped his backpack closed, left the library,

and walked down the hallway to the nearest boys' bathroom. He set his backpack on one of the sinks and had barely unzipped it an inch when a furry brown head peeked out.

A furry brown rat head.

Its eyes were black. Its whiskers twitched. It bobbed its head from side to side. Unlike the rats from the first day of school, this one seemed friendly. Maybe even playful.

Robert opened the zipper a little more and a second head emerged. This one had the same brown fur, the same black eyes.

Twins, Robert thought.

Like the red-haired girls in his science class.

Somehow the rats must have climbed into his backpack while he was talking with Karina. Robert unzipped it all the way, planning to shake them loose and set them free. But as they stepped out, Robert realized he was mistaken—these were not twins.

This was a single rat with two heads.

"Whoa," Robert whispered. "What *are* you guys?"

Both heads looked up and squealed. They shared the same torso, the same feet, and the same tail. One of them brushed its neck against Robert's wrist. It wanted to be petted!

"All right," he said, stroking the backs of their necks with his finger. "You like that? Does that feel good?"

Clearly it did. The two heads closed their eyes and purred like baby kittens.

"How about water? Are you thirsty?"

He turned on one of the faucets and made a cup with his hand. The rats stepped lightly onto the sink and lapped the water from his palm. The two tiny tongues felt like tabs of sandpaper against Robert's skin.

"There you go," Robert whispered. "Take your time and drink up. That's a good boy—er, boys."

Just then, the bathroom door banged open.

The rats leapt from the sink into the backpack and Robert quickly zipped it closed.

Glenn Torkells stood in the doorway, grinning at Robert.

"Dweeb tax, Nerdbert," he said, holding out his

palm. "You know you're not supposed to use the bathroom on Fridays."

It was another of Glenn's stupid rules.

"Fine," Robert said. He moved the backpack out of Glenn's reach before taking two dollars from his pocket. "Here you go. All right? No problem."

Glenn pocketed the money and stared at him.

And smiled.

"What are you so nervous about?"

"Nothing," Robert said, glancing down at his backpack, relieved to see it wasn't moving. Somehow the rats seemed to understand that they needed to remain very still.

"You're not your usual self today, Nerdbert. I can tell. I've got a real good memory."

"I paid your stupid tax, all right? Leave me alone."

Robert grabbed his backpack and tried to leave, but Glenn blocked his way.

"What's in your bag?"

"Nothing. Books."

"Let me see."

Glenn reached for the bag and Robert tried stepping around him, but he wasn't fast enough. Glenn grabbed a shoulder strap and yanked hard, pulling Robert along with it.

"Careful!" Robert shouted.

"Careful of what?" Glenn asked.

"None of your business! Leave me alone!"

At times like these, Robert thought of the characters in his favorite books—the supposedly normal kids who possessed secret powers. Robert wished he had eyeball lasers that could fry Glenn to a crisp. He wished he could summon a giant beast that would drag Glenn away kicking and screaming.

But this wasn't a fantasy novel. This was real life.

Glenn grabbed Robert's wrist and twisted it behind his back, then shoved his face against the wall. "Here's what's going to happen, Nerdbert. I'm going to keep twisting your arm until you let go of your backpack. Do you understand me?"

"Enough!" shouted a deep voice.

Robert looked to the door of the restroom and

saw Mr. Loomis charging toward them.

Glenn released his grip.

"Principal's office," Mr. Loomis told him. "Now."

"But I was just playing—"

"Now!" Mr. Loomis's voice boomed off the walls. Maybe he never shouted in English class, but here in the boys' bathroom it was clear he meant business.

Glenn flashed Robert a dirty look. "I've got a real good memory," he warned, before stomping out the door.

Mr. Loomis knelt beside Robert. "Are you all right?"

Robert shook out his arm. "I'm fine."

"Does Glenn pick on you a lot?"

"Not really."

Mr. Loomis frowned. "This was the first time?"

Robert shrugged. "Yeah."

The 12:30 bell rang. Normally it would be time for lunch but today there was an early dismissal. Outside the bathroom, the hallway was filled with the noise of kids opening lockers and chatting about their weekends.

"So, can I go now?" Robert asked.

Mr. Loomis studied his face, as if he were literally searching for the truth. "Robert, you need to be focused on your schoolwork. Not worrying about bullies. I can make this problem go away, but I need you to tell me what's going on."

It was the opportunity Robert had been waiting for. Here was a teacher willing to listen and capable of stopping Glenn once and for all. And yet Robert was too ashamed to tell him the truth.

Boys were supposed to stand up for themselves. If Robert told Mr. Loomis everything—if he told him about the gummy worms and the dweeb tax and all the name-calling—he knew he would sound pathetic. It was too humiliating.

He could feel the creatures in his backpack squirming, getting restless.

"There's no problem," Robert said. "Can I go now?"

CHAPTER
SEVEN

He ran all the way home, bolted upstairs to his bedroom, kicked off his sneakers, lay down on his bed, and gently unzipped his backpack.

The two heads emerged—first one, then the other—and inquisitively sniffed the bedroom air. "Come on out, little guys," he said. "You're totally safe here. This is my room. No jerks allowed."

The rats stepped cautiously onto the blankets. Robert petted their necks and soon they were purring again, happy to be lounging on his bed.

"Now first things first," he said. "You need a name."

He'd considered all kinds of options while racing

home—he thought Double Jeopardy sounded the coolest—but decided that he needed to pick two names. One for the left head, and one for the right.

Mario and Luigi?

Phineas and Ferb?

Stars and Stripes?

None of them seemed quite right. And then inspiration struck. He addressed the rats one at a time, first the left head and then the right. "You're going to be Pip, and you're going to be Squeak. Together, you're Pipsqueak!"

The rats seemed to love it. In fact, Squeak squeaked his approval several times, as if trying to prove he understood Robert's decision.

"Now stay here," Robert said, "while I get some food."

He ran downstairs to the kitchen, where his mother was standing over the stove, stirring a pot of soup. "There you are!" she exclaimed. "How was your day, sweetie?"

"Good."

"What are you doing?"

Robert was already inside the refrigerator and loading his arms with two apples, a brick of cheese, a handful of lettuce, and a bag of baby carrots. "Just grabbing a snack. Thanks, Mom. Call me when dinner's ready, okay?"

In a flash he was back on his bed, sharing the food with Pip and Squeak. Clearly they were hungry; they leapt upon the apple, gripping it with their claws and gnawing it to the core. Robert watched them, mesmerized. Each head moved independently of the other; sometimes Pip would eat while Squeak rested, and vice versa.

The food was gone in just ten minutes. Pip and Squeak looked to Robert with pleading eyes. "I'll bring more after dinner," he told them. "If I do it now, my mom will be suspicious." Robert knew his mother wouldn't tolerate a pet rat in the house, let alone a two-headed mutation.

He found a cardboard box in his closet, then shredded the pages of an old loose-leaf notebook, arranging the scraps of paper into a sort of nest. Then he placed a small bowl of water in one corner. "This is where you'll sleep at night," he explained.

Pip and Squeak grasped the idea immediately. They climbed up into the box, settled into a corner, smiled at Robert, and chattered their teeth. It was a weird clicking noise that seemed to indicate they were happy.

"You guys are going to be nice and cozy here," he promised. "And it's Friday, so we've got all weekend to play. Maybe we'll go in the backyard tomorrow, would you like that?"

There was a sudden knock at the door.

"Robert? Can I come in?"

He grabbed the box and shoved it under the bed.

"It's open!" he called.

His mother entered the room. "Did you just get off the phone?" Robert shook his head. "I thought I heard you talking to someone."

"Must have been the radio."

It was clear Mrs. Arthur didn't believe him. She sat beside him on the bed and wrapped her arm around his waist.

"Is everything all right?"

"Yeah."

"You like the new school?"

"Yeah."

"Are you having any problems?"

"Yeah. I mean, no."

His mother looked down at him. "I'm trying to have a conversation, Robert. Do you understand? This doesn't work unless you're actively listening and sharing information."

"I'm sorry," Robert said.

And he truly was sorry. His mother already had enough problems, between working full shifts at the hospital and cooking and cleaning and doing all the laundry. She never had any time leftover for going out and doing anything fun. The least he could do was cheer her up a little.

"Lovecraft is fantastic," he told her. "We went to the library today? For the first time? And you wouldn't believe it, Mom. It's so big, I actually got lost."

She smiled. "Seriously?"

"Yeah, and my English teacher? Mr. Loomis? He's this really nice guy. He showed me where to check out books. Oh, and I made a new friend today!"

"Really? That's wonderful!"

"Two new friends, actually," Robert said, smiling as he thought of Pip and Squeak underneath his bed, their whiskered snouts just inches away from his mother's delicate ankles.

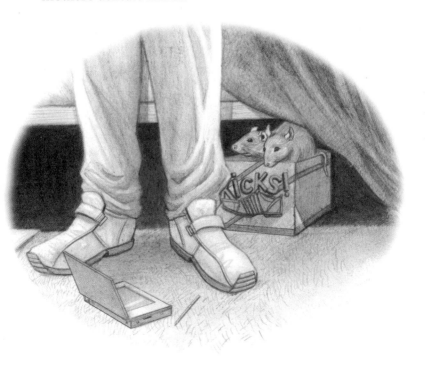

CHAPTER EIGHT

Robert spent most of the weekend playing with his new friends. During the day, he brought them to his neighborhood park. At night, they stayed up late together, eating snacks by flashlight under the blankets. Pip favored chocolate cupcakes with white filling. Squeak preferred peanut butter cookies. They both loved hard pretzels and scattered crumbs all over Robert's sheets.

Their intelligence was extraordinary. After just a few hours, Robert had trained them to obey simple commands such as "sit" and "stay" and "roll over." By Sunday night, they were executing even more complicated tasks. "Bring me a comic book," Robert would say. And Pip and Squeak dutifully walked over to his shelves, retrieved a comic book, and carried it in their mouths back to their master.

Robert rewarded them with more pretzels. "Two heads are definitely better than one," he said, gently stroking their necks and back. "You guys are twice as smart as the average rat. Maybe even smarter."

He went online to research two-headed animals. They were a lot more common than he'd realized. He found photographs of two-headed cows, two-headed pigs, even a two-headed crocodile. The scientific name for the condition was *polycephaly*. Robert found several articles about polycephaly in medical journals, but they were all too complicated for him to understand. Yet one of them caught his attention because its author, Crawford Tillinghast, lived right there in Dunwich, Massachusetts, just a mile or two from Robert's house.

Robert walked downstairs to the living room, where his mother was folding laundry on the sofa. "Hey, did you ever hear of a man named Crawford Tillinghast?"

"Sure," she said. "You remember that giant mansion on East Chestnut Street? The one they finally knocked down last year? That's where he lived. He was some kind of scientist."

"Does he still live in Dunwich?"

"Oh, no, honey. He died thirty years ago. There was a house fire, I think. Why do you ask?"

Robert shrugged. "No reason."

His mother laughed. "When I was real little, we used to joke that his house was haunted. You'd go out there at night and see all kinds of crazy lights flashing in his windows. We used to dare one another to run up his steps and ring the doorbell. Poor old man."

Upstairs, something toppled over with a crash. It sounded like Pip and Squeak had found their way into Robert's closet.

"What was that?" his mother asked.

"Nothing," he assured her. "Just some books falling off my bed. I'll go take care of it."

When Robert returned to his room, Pip and Squeak were hiding in their nest box, their heads buried under the paper scraps. "You need to be quiet when I'm not here," he warned them. "Do you understand me? If my mother finds you, she will freak out."

Pip squeaked and Squeak bobbed his head, so Robert wished them a good night and pushed the box back under the bed.

When he woke the next morning, the box was empty.

Robert leapt out of bed. He searched under his bed, inside his closet, even in his desk drawers. Since his mother had already left for the day, Robert was free to run about the house, shouting their names. "Pip! Squeak! Pip and Squeak!" But there was no sign of them.

He remembered what Professor Goyle had taught him: A rat's jaws were powerful enough to chew through brick, concrete, or lead pipe. A rat could squeeze through spaces as narrow as a half inch. It wouldn't have been hard for Pip and Squeak to escape the house. Maybe Robert hurt their feelings when he reprimanded them the night before. Maybe they decided to go live somewhere else.

He ate a quiet breakfast at the kitchen table, brushed his teeth, and then grabbed his backpack, ready to walk out the door. Then he felt a familiar weight shifting inside the bag. He unzipped the main pouch and there they were, Pip and Squeak, grinning up at him.

"You want to come with me?" he asked. "Back to school?"

Pip nodded. Squeak chattered his teeth.

Robert didn't like the idea. He hadn't thought about Glenn Torkells all weekend—his new pets had been a nice distraction—but he knew the bully would want revenge.

"You have to promise me you'll be absolutely quiet," he told them. "No squirming around. If anyone notices something screwy, I won't be able to protect you."

Pip and Squeak seemed happy with this arrangement. Robert zipped them into his backpack and headed out the front door.

Lovecraft Middle School was an eight-block walk from his house. When Robert arrived on campus, he immediately saw that something was wrong. In the parking lot were five police cars and two news vans. Over by the bike rack, a television reporter was holding a microphone and addressing the camera about "a terrible tragedy that's rocked this quiet little community."

Robert quickened his pace, approaching the main entrance. The large digital screen beside the front doors had a new message:

MISSING STUDENT

Seventh-grader Sylvia Price has been reported
missing. If you have any information, please
tell a teacher or dial 911.

Next to the words was a photograph of a young girl
with long red hair. Robert recognized her as one of the
twins from Professor Goyle's class.

For the rest of the day, it was hard for Robert to
concentrate on anything else. The hallways were filled
with hearsay and gossip. Sylvia had run away to live in
New York City. Sylvia was abducted by a hitchhiker.
Sylvia was last seen walking in the woods behind Lovecraft Middle School. The truth was anybody's guess.

Most of Robert's teachers were upset by the news,
and Mr. Loomis seemed genuinely angry. "You kids
need to use common sense!" he said, stomping around
his classroom in a lime-green sweater vest. "Don't talk
to strangers! Watch where you walk at night! Be careful around people and places you don't know!"

Robert knew all this already. Teachers had been

warning him about stranger danger since he was five years old. But everyone in his class listened without protest. They understood that Mr. Loomis was simply frustrated, that he was trying to prevent a terrible thing from happening again.

At lunchtime, Robert went outside to the athletic stadium and shared a ham sandwich with Pip and Squeak. They were relieved to be out of the backpack and they ran the length of the bleachers, zigzagging up and down, over and over. Robert stood guard, making sure no teachers or students were watching them.

"You guys have been real good all day," he told his pets. "You stay nice and quiet, and we're going to be just fine."

When Robert arrived in science, the desks on both sides of him were empty. His classmates explained that Sarah Price was home with her family, helping the police investigate Sylvia's disappearance. The mood in the class was unusually quiet. Even the caged animals in the back of the room seemed more silent than normal.

Professor Goyle arrived as if it were just another day, dropping his leather satchel onto his desk and turning to the chalkboard. "We're going to pick up where we left off on Friday," he explained, drawing the outline of a human skull on the chalkboard. "There are eight different bones in the cranium, and anyone who wants to pass this class is going to memorize all of them."

Suddenly he turned around and wrinkled his nose. "What's that hideous odor?"

Robert and his classmates exchanged glances. What was he talking about? The classroom smelled just like it always had.

Lynn Scott, one of the girls in the front row, raised her hand. "Professor Goyle? Are you going to say anything about Sylvia Price?"

He arched his bushy eyebrows. "Sylvia who?"

Lynn pointed at the empty chair. "The girl who went missing last night."

"Ah, yes. The monozygotic twin."

Professor Goyle sat on his desk and folded his

hands in his lap, as if he were preparing to comfort the class with a bedtime story. "I understand that many of you are upset. It's unfortunate when a child goes missing. But we must remember, students, that everything happens for a reason. There are forces in this world you cannot comprehend. The Great Old Ones have the intelligence of ten thousand men combined. We should not question their actions—but what on earth is that *horrible* fetid odor?"

Goyle marched up and down the aisles of the classroom, twitching his nose like a bloodhound on the trail of a scent. "It's absolutely *revolting*!" he exclaimed. "I can't believe any of you can concentrate with this hideous *stench* in the air!" He stopped beside Robert's desk, then knelt down, pressed his face against Robert's backpack, and breathed in deeply. "What's in this bag, Mr. Arthur?"

"N-n-nothing," Robert stammered. "Just my gym clothes?"

"I sincerely doubt *that*," Professor Goyle said. He unzipped the backpack, reached inside, and pulled out

Pip and Squeak by the napes of their necks. Both heads squeaked helplessly as their feet swayed in the air. The other students in the classroom gasped.

"A polycephalous rodent? Where did you find this horrible two-headed mutation?"

Robert's classmates all leaned forward for a better look while he struggled to answer the question. "Um, in the library?"

"Where in the library?"

"In the attic? Above the library?"

Goyle's eyes widened. "An attic above the library?" This seemed to strike him as a revelation. "That's very interesting, Mr. Arthur. But Lovecraft Middle School has very strict rules forbidding pets. If you'd read your student handbook, you would know this!"

"I'm sorry," Robert said. "Please, Professor. I promise I'll bring them home tonight, and I won't bring them to school again."

Goyle shook his head. "That wouldn't be safe. We've already discussed the dangers of rats. Don't you remember the lessons of the Black Death? Weren't you paying attention?"

"Pip and Squeak are different. They're friendly."

"They're diseased! They're filthy! And a two-headed mutation could be twice as dangerous. I can't let you take this monstrosity home with you." Goyle walked to the rear of the classroom, holding Pip and Squeak at a distance, as if any physical contact posed a health risk.

Robert's classmates watched, fascinated, as Goyle dropped Pip and Squeak in a small aquarium lined with wood shavings, then closed the top with a metal lid. "They'll be safe in here until I can dispose of them."

The other students cheered as if Goyle had done something heroic, as if he'd just vanquished a hideous monster. Goyle resumed his lecture, but Robert could barely concentrate. The rest of the class passed in a blur.

When the end-of-day bell rang, Robert trudged back to his locker. He wasn't in any hurry to go home. Or to go anywhere, really. All he could think about were Pip and Squeak, trapped in the aquarium at the back of Professor Goyle's classroom.

How was Goyle going to "dispose" of them?

Did that mean what Robert thought it meant?

He considered going to his mother or even Mr. Loomis for help, but he knew they wouldn't understand. Rules were rules. Pets weren't allowed on school property and wild two-headed rats couldn't be trusted. If his mother saw Pip and Squeak, she wouldn't rush to their defense; she would scream.

When Robert closed his locker, he discovered Karina standing alongside him, chewing gum and clutching her skateboard.

"Bummer about your pet," she said. "Goyle can be a real jerk."

"How'd you hear?" he asked.

"News travels fast."

"They're friendly animals, I swear," Robert explained. "I played with them all weekend. They slept in a box under my bed. Pip and Squeak wouldn't hurt anyone, I know them." His voice was trembling. He was so upset, he was afraid he might start crying, right there in the hallway, right in front of a girl.

"I believe you, Robert."

"Goyle said he was going to dispose of them. What do you think that means? 'Dispose of them'?"

Karina smiled. "I think it means we need to steal them back."

That night after dinner, Robert's mother did something she hadn't done in a long time: She went upstairs, put on some dressy clothes, and prepared for an evening on the town. It was Parent-Teacher Night, and she'd been looking forward to it all week.

"How do I look?" she asked. She was wearing a fancy black dress and fake pearls. She'd even put on makeup. Robert was sitting on the couch, watching television.

"You know the president's not going to be there, right?" he asked.

Her shoulders slumped. "I thought I looked nice."

"You do," he said quickly. "I'm sorry."

"Well, I better get going. Don't want to be late. I should be home around nine or so. Maybe later. Don't spend all night watching TV, okay?"

That won't be a problem, he thought.

As soon as she drove away, Robert grabbed his backpack and proceeded to follow her on foot.

Earlier that afternoon, Karina had explained that tonight was the best possible time to retrieve Pip and Squeak. If Goyle was planning to "dispose" of them, there wasn't a minute to waste. And thanks to Parent-Teacher Night, the doors of Lovecraft Middle School would be open long after dark. It was a rare opportunity to sneak into a classroom without being discovered.

Robert jogged the eight blocks to the school in just a few minutes. He needed to be quick. He wanted to rescue Pip and Squeak and get home before his mother returned, so she'd never know he snuck out.

When he arrived at the school, he saw dozens of parents walking into the main entrance. The orientation would take place in the central auditorium, far from the east wing of the second floor and Professor Goyle's classroom.

Karina was waiting where they'd agreed to meet, just inside the entrance to the east wing. Here, the hallway lights were dimmed. All of the classrooms were dark.

"Are you ready?" she asked.

"I guess," he said. "Have you seen anyone?"

"The coast is clear. Come on."

He followed along, wondering how a girl who claimed to be afraid of spiders could be so fearless about breaking into a teacher's classroom. He'd never met anyone quite like Karina Ortiz.

They climbed the stairs to the second floor and arrived at the entrance to Room 213. For a brief moment, Robert feared the door might be locked. But when he tried the knob, it turned easily in his grip.

The classroom seemed eerie in the dark. All those empty desks. The grinning skeleton at the front of the classroom. But Robert didn't dare turn on the lights.

"Where are they?" Karina asked.

Robert led her to the back of the classroom, past the tropical fish and the lizards, until he arrived at the tank containing Pip and Squeak. His pets jumped up, delighted, pressing their paws against the glass. Robert tried to remove the lid but it wouldn't budge.

"Is it locked?" Karina asked.

"I think it's stuck."

He felt under the lid, looking for some kind of button or latch. But the metal had a fine smooth edge all the way around. Robert grabbed and pulled as hard as he could. It was like trying to pry open a can of tuna fish with his bare hands. Impossible.

Next, he tried lifting the aquarium off the shelf. It weighed probably twenty pounds. He could carry it out of the school if he had to. He could pry off the lid when he got home, maybe use a screwdriver . . .

"Listen!" Karina whispered. "Someone's coming!"

Robert heard the footsteps, too. Out in the hallway and approaching fast. He and Karina darted around the classroom, looking for a place to hide. Under the teacher's desk? Behind the skeleton?

"Supply closet!" Karina said.

Robert ran to the open door on the side of the classroom. It was here that Goyle stored his extra beakers and test tubes and chemistry supplies. Karina entered first and it didn't look like there was enough room for both of them.

"I won't fit," Robert said.

"Just get in here!"

He pulled the door closed just as the classroom overhead lights flickered on. Somehow they both fit inside.

"Shhh," Karina whispered. "Don't move."

Robert was too scared to reply. He heard about a party game called Seven Minutes in Heaven, in which a boy and a girl would go into a closet for seven minutes and . . . well, he wasn't exactly sure what they did. Hug? Kiss? He wondered if it was something like this.

The closet door was slightly ajar, allowing them a narrow view into the classroom. Professor Goyle was carrying a jug of water and a sack of food pellets. He brought them to the back of the classroom and proceeded to feed all the animals. He hummed a strange little melody as he worked—then stopped when he reached the tank containing Pip and Squeak.

"What's that? You're hungry, too? Ha!" Goyle laughed. "You're being punished for trying to escape. For sneaking into that boy's backpack. What if an adult had seen you? Can you imagine the consequences? This whole plan, everything Master has designed, it would all come tumbling down! *Shub-niggurath! K'hala dorsath f'ah!*"

Robert wasn't sure he'd heard that last part correctly. Was Goyle simply mumbling? The words had sounded clear, yet they were in a language that was wholly unfamiliar.

"Master wants to see you both in the morning. Until then he's asked me to give you a message."

Goyle reached into the adjacent tank and removed a brown-and-white hamster by the nape of its neck. "Watch carefully," he told Pip and Squeak. "This is what will happen if you attempt another escape."

Goyle raised the hamster high above his head. The animal swung its paws wildly, desperate to scramble away, but Goyle's grip was too strong. He opened his mouth, as though threatening to eat the animal.

It was just a dumb, cruel stunt, Robert thought. The same kind of mean prank that Glenn Torkells seemed to enjoy. Goyle was just another bully.

Then there was a hideous snapping sound, and the bottom half of Goyle's jaw collapsed. It fell open like the mouth of a ventriloquist's dummy, revealing sharp white fangs and a gaping black maw. Goyle lowered the hamster between his lips and swallowed it whole.

Robert felt dizzy, like he was going to pass out. The walls of the closet were spinning. He grabbed a shelf to steady himself.

"Stay calm," Karina whispered. "Don't make a sound."

Goyle stroked the top of his chest, coaxing the hamster down his digestive tract. Then he uncapped the jug of water, took a long drink, and burped.

"Let that be a warning to you," he told Pip and Squeak. "I'll bring you to see Master in the morning."

A minute later, the classroom went dark again and

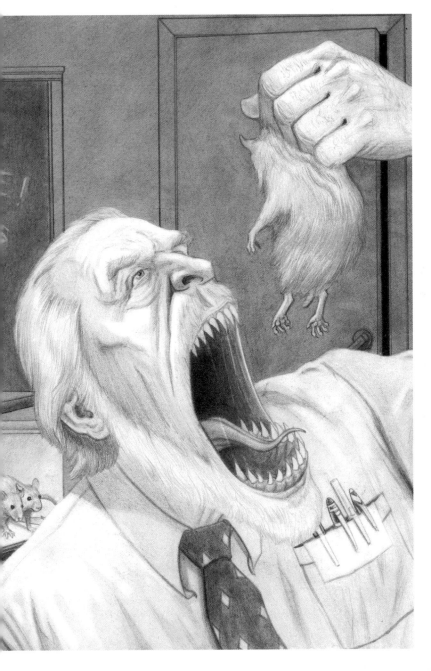

Robert heard Goyle close the door and leave.

"What just happened?" he whispered.

"We nearly got caught is what happened," Karina said. "We're lucky."

"Do you think he's really gone?"

"It's fine. Get us out of here."

Robert opened the door. His brain was screaming for him to run but he couldn't leave without Pip and Squeak. Not after what he'd just seen.

"You'll have to carry the aquarium," Karina said.

"Too heavy," Robert said. "If Goyle sees us? And chases us? Forget it."

He would have to take more drastic measures. He opened the classroom door and peered into the hallway. Still empty. There was no sign of Goyle, and all the parents and teachers were in the auditorium on the far side of the school.

Robert returned to the back of the classroom and unzipped his backpack. "Get ready to run," he told Karina.

"What are you going to do?"

He tapped on the side of the aquarium. Pip and Squeak stood up against the glass, like they were trying to smell his fingertips. "Hang on tight, guys. There's only one way to get you out of here, but it's going to be a little bumpy."

Robert tilted the aquarium on one side and let it topple off the shelf, landing with a crash. Glass shards and wood shavings exploded in all directions. Pip and Squeak leapt from the blast and landed with a tumble inside Robert's backpack.

"Let's go!" Karina cried.

They raced out of the classroom, stopping just long enough to close the door behind them. No one was chasing them, but Robert wasn't taking any chances. He ran like a madman down the hallway, down the stairwell, and out the door of the east entrance. He looked back and saw Karina hesitating inside the school.

"What are you waiting for?" he asked. "Come on!"

"I'm going the other way," she said, pointing down the hallway toward the west entrance. "I live on the other side of town."

"What are we going to do about Goyle?"

"We can talk tomorrow. Meet me in the attic."

"Be careful," he said. "Make sure no one sees you."

Robert ran all the way home. There was so much to think about, so much he didn't understand. *Why was Professor Goyle speaking to Pip and Squeak like they could actually understand him? Where had they escaped from? Who was this Master he kept talking about?* None of it made any sense.

When he returned home, he fixed Pip and Squeak a big dinner of roasted ham, raisin bran, celery, grapes, and a half dozen hard pretzels. They tore through the food in minutes, and then Robert ushered them into their nest and put them to bed.

Ten minutes later, his mother's car pulled into the driveway. She entered the house looking exhilarated, like she'd just returned from the greatest party of her life.

"Unbelievable!" she exclaimed. "Did you know you can start taking Mandarin Chinese in eighth grade? Did you know Mr. Loomis has a master's degree from Yale University? Did you know the school was built from all these different recycled materials?"

"You liked it?" Robert asked.

She swept him up in her arms. "I loved it, sweetie. It's such a wonderful school. I'm so happy for you. Happy for us." Her smile faltered. "Though it's a real shame about that missing girl, Sylvia Price. All the parents were talking about the investigation. Did you know her?"

"Not really."

"I hope they find her soon. I can't imagine what her family's going through. Your science teacher—I think his name was Mr. Goyle? He told us all not to worry. He said he was confident Sylvia would come home."

At the mention of Goyle, Robert remembered how his teacher had unhinged his jaw like a boa constrictor and then pushed a live hamster into his mouth.

"He seemed nice," Robert's mother added.

CHAPTER TEN

When Robert woke the next morning, Pip and Squeak were waiting in his backpack, apparently ready to return to Lovecraft Middle School.

"Are you kidding me?" he asked. "Did you hear *anything* Goyle said yesterday? Remember how he smelled you through my backpack? Remember the hamster?"

Pip and Squeak nodded their heads as if they shared all of Robert's concerns. But when he reached into the backpack, they squirmed away, avoiding his grasp.

"Guys, this is crazy. You're not safe at Lovecraft. You

need to stay here until I figure out what's going on."

Pip and Squeak shook their heads. They seemed determined to return to the school—to follow Robert wherever he went—but he couldn't understand why.

"Fine, suit yourselves," he said, zipping up the backpack and slinging it over his shoulder. "But you're staying in my locker during science."

It had just started raining when Robert arrived at school, and his morning classes seemed to last for hours. He couldn't concentrate on anything besides the events of the previous evening. He could remember exactly what Goyle had said to Pip and Squeak:

What if an adult had seen you? Can you imagine the consequences?

This whole plan, everything Master has designed, it would all come tumbling down.

Shub-niggurath! K'hala dorsath f'ah!

What the heck did it all mean?

After what seemed like a hundred million hours,

the lunch bell finally rang. Robert was just leaving English class when Mr. Loomis stopped him.

"Hey, Robert? Got a second?"

"Yeah?"

"Is everything all right? I noticed you weren't paying attention in class today. You seem like you're worried about something."

Robert imagined telling the truth: "*Last night I snuck into the school after dark and watched Professor Goyle swallow a hamster.*"

It wasn't going to fly.

"Everything's fine, Mr. Loomis. I'm just a little tired."

"And that boy Glenn? Is he still bothering you?"

"No, he leaves me alone," Robert said. "Can I go now?"

"All right," Mr. Loomis said. "Just checking."

Robert bypassed the cafeteria and went straight to the library. Eating lunch wasn't nearly as important as getting to the attic and talking to Karina about last night.

He paced up and down the aisles of the fiction section, trying to retrace his steps from the previous week. He found the paranormal mystery section but couldn't find his way to the attic. *I turned left here, then right here, then right again. Or was it left?* Robert looked for a corner that was shrouded in shadows; he remembered it was hard to see. Today, he could not see it at all.

Finally he approached Ms. Lavinia at the circulation desk. She was waving a paperback book under the red glow of a bar-code scanner.

"Hello, young man. Can I help you?"

"I'm trying to find that room with the old books? At the top of the stairs?"

Ms. Lavinia peered over her cat-eye glasses. "Did you say old books?"

"Yeah, big leather-bound books. Some of them look like they're two hundred years old."

"You must be thinking of the town library," she said. "All of our books are brand-new. We received a very generous donation from a charitable foundation."

Robert shook his head. "I know it's right over there," he said, pointing toward the fiction shelves. "It looks like an attic. You can see rafters and everything. One of the doors is nailed shut with planks."

Ms. Lavinia stared back at him in astonishment.

"Young man," she said, "I have no idea what you're talking about."

CHAPTER ELEVEN

In the minutes between sixth and seventh periods, Robert stashed Pip and Squeak on the top shelf of his locker. "Now stay here and be quiet," he told them. "Science is my last class of the day, and then I'll come back to get you."

He was preparing for the worst. He knew Professor Goyle would be furious, that he'd be looking for the person who broke his aquarium and freed Pip and Squeak. And Robert was the most likely suspect. He didn't think Goyle would threaten him in a classroom full of witnesses. But what if Goyle told Robert to stay behind after class? What would happen then?

It was tempting to skip the class altogether, but Robert worried that doing so would make him look even guiltier. He decided he would go to class and act like he'd had nothing to do with it. Maybe the rats had simply overturned the aquarium on their own. That was possible, wasn't it?

Robert was one of the last students to arrive in the classroom. Someone had cleaned up the broken glass and shavings. There was no sign of any disturbance. But at least one other student noticed that Pip and Squeak were gone.

"Hey, Nerdbert!" Glenn called from across the room. "Looks like Goyle got rid of your pet!"

Robert ignored him, sat down, and took out a notebook. He began to recopy his homework in neater handwriting. He wanted to be busy working when Goyle arrived, so he'd have an excuse for not making eye contact.

But the late bell rang and still no teacher came.

The skeleton at the front of the classroom appeared to be watching the door, as if it was waiting for a teacher like everyone else. Robert was reminded of the first day of school, when Sarah Price suggested that Robert go to the principal's office and get help. It was only two weeks ago, but it seemed like ancient history.

Finally, the classroom door opened and in walked a short, stout woman with thick glasses and curly black hair. The students gawked as she carried a stack of folders over to Professor Goyle's desk.

"Good afternoon, everyone. My name is Mrs. Kinski and I'll be your substitute teacher this afternoon. It seems poor Professor Goyle has an upset stomach today."

Again, Robert recalled the image of Goyle with his jaw unhinged, stuffing a live hamster into his mouth.

"Now pay attention, because I have some exciting news," Mrs. Kinski continued. "For today's lesson, we're going to look at a strange world that's teeming with thousands of bizarre species. You'll be shocked to learn that this world is waiting just outside the doors of this school. In fact, it's so close, you kids could bike over and dip your toes in it." As she spoke, Mrs. Kinski lowered a projection screen at the front of the classroom. It was filled with images of a rolling blue sea. "I'm talking about the ocean, of course, and today we're going to watch a documentary about the exciting field of marine biology!"

A couple of kids clapped, but the rest had already started passing notes or goofing off. Robert had never been so grateful to have a substitute teacher. He hoped Mrs. Kinski would teach Goyle's class all week.

At 2:45, the last bell rang and Robert returned to the library. He spent another twenty minutes trying to find his way back to the attic, without success. Ms. Lavinia watched him skeptically from her chair at the circulation desk. "We'll be closing in ten minutes," she told him. "There's always the public library, if you need more time."

Robert walked to his locker. By this time, all his classmates were gone; all the hallways were empty; all the digital bulletin boards were already turned off for the night.

His footsteps echoed across the tiled floor.

He stopped in front of his locker, entered the combination, and opened the door.

"Squeak? Pip? Where are you guys?"

The top shelf was empty except for *Fangs Dungaree* and the large leather-bound book that Robert had taken from the attic. There was no sign of his pets. Robert panicked, tearing through the pile of the books at the bottom of his locker. Finally he noticed that the hood of his windbreaker was moving; he peered inside and there were Pip and Squeak, cozied up as if they were resting in a hammock.

"There you are!" he exclaimed. "You guys scared me!"

"Who scared you?" Glenn Torkells asked.

He had come out of nowhere. Robert tried to swing the locker door closed but he wasn't fast enough; Glenn blocked it with his big, dirty boot.

"I asked you a question, Nerdbert. Who scared you?" Glenn peered into the locker, but Pip and Squeak had burrowed even deeper into the hood of the windbreaker.

"Nobody," Robert said. "I was just talking to myself."

Glenn laughed. "So you scared yourself? You're such a chicken you actually scared yourself? I should charge you a double dweeb tax for that one."

Robert grabbed the windbreaker and tucked it beneath his arm. "I have to go."

"Hang on a second," Glenn said, reaching into the locker for the leather-bound book. "Where'd you get this thing? From one of those Halloween stores?" Glenn opened the cover and dust fell from the pages. He pointed to an illustration of an old man with a single horn in the center of his head. "Who's this," he asked, pointing at it with a dirty fingernail, "your dad?"

"Very funny," Robert said. "Give it back."

"Hang on a second," Glenn said, "I'm going to tell you a story." He flipped to a passage in the middle of the book. "*Deph-pha. Ctzelzog. Enorhula-tu.*" He was stumbling over the words; they were impossible to pronounce. "Is this French or something? Who talks this way?"

"Just give it back," Robert pleaded.

"Hey, listen to this one. *Kyaloh yog-sothoth f'ah. Kyaloh yog-sothoth f'ah.*" He bobbed his head like he was rapping to a beat box. "*Ky-ky-kyaloh. Yo-yo-yog-sothoth.*"

Robert became aware of a cold draft coming from his locker. It was weird; it felt like the temperature in the hallway had abruptly dropped thirty degrees. And there was a smell, too. A strangely familiar smell. Like moldy mothballs. The draft was stronger now, an actual gust of wind—but how was that possible?

"*Ky-ky-kyaloh—*"

"Glenn," Robert said.

"*Yo-yo-yog-sothoth—*"

"Glenn, I think you should stop," Robert said. As he spoke, puffs of white vapor left his mouth, like he was outdoors in the middle of January. An icy frost was forming on the edges of the book, as though it had suddenly frozen solid.

"Yow!" Glenn exclaimed, dropping the book to the floor. "What's wrong with that thing?"

"I don't think you should have read that."

Robert tried to pick up the book, but it was so cold it burned his fingertips. He yanked his hand away.

The wind was making his locker buckle and stretch; it seemed to be widening, almost yawning. The back wall of the locker had dissolved into a sort of swirling blackness. Robert stared into the center of the spiral. There was something hypnotic about it. He might have kept staring if Glenn hadn't tugged on his arm, yanking him back to the present.

"Hey, what is that?"

Robert looked down. Extending from the locker and coiled around Glenn's left ankle was a purple and yellow tentacle. Like the arm of a giant octopus, minus the suckers. Its surface glistened with slime.

The tentacle tugged on Glenn's leg.

"Whoa!" Glenn shouted, shifting off-balance suddenly, hopping on his one free leg and struggling to stand upright. "What the heck, man! Get it off!"

Robert reached down but there was no place to grip the tentacle; his hands slipped helplessly over its slimy surface. "I'll get a teacher."

"No!" Glenn shouted. The tentacle tugged again, pulling Glenn closer to the locker, pulling his right leg *inside* the locker. "Don't leave me here, Robert!" Glenn grabbed the sides of the locker to steady himself, but more tentacles were tethering themselves around his arms and wrists and waist. "Come on, help me! I'm losing my grip!"

Robert hated Glenn more than anyone he'd met in his entire life, but what else could he do? No one deserved this. Whatever *this* was. He swung his leg with all his might, kicking one of the tentacles. It didn't budge.

Another tentacle slithered out of the locker and grabbed Glenn's right ankle, yanking his leg into the black vortex. He was off the ground now, hanging on for his life, nearly consumed. Robert reached out and grabbed Glenn's wrists, trying to pull him out, but he was no match for the beast beyond the locker.

"Don't let go!" Glenn yelled, his eyes wide with terror. "Please, Robert, don't you let—" And then a thin purple tentacle coiled itself around Glenn's mouth, silencing his voice.

Robert could feel Glenn's wrists slipping through his fingers. It was too late. He was losing his grip and Glenn was going to disappear inside the black, swirling vortex . . .

And then Robert felt four tiny paws racing up his back and vaulting over his shoulder. Pip and Squeak landed on the largest tentacle and sank their teeth into it. From deep within the locker came a low, bellowing roar. Pip and Squeak bit again and again. Fizzy green goo bubbled out of the wounds like a strange toxic sludge. One by one, the tentacles released their grip on Glenn and retreated into the locker. Robert pulled hard on Glenn's wrists, yanking him back into the hallway. Both boys landed in a heap on the floor and for a long time, at least a minute, they didn't move. They were too numb and frightened and exhausted to do anything.

The next time Robert looked at his locker, it resembled a perfectly ordinary locker, with rigid metal walls and a hook for hanging coats. Pip and Squeak were resting contentedly on the small shelf near the top.

"What just happened?" Glenn finally asked.

"We saved your life," Robert said. "You're supposed to say thank you."

TWELVE

Robert stepped through the front door of his house and called out to his mother. "Mom, are you here?"

"In the kitchen," she called back.

"I brought a friend for dinner, is that okay?"

"You brought a *what*?"

Glenn lingered in the doorway, as if he hadn't made up his mind to stay or go. "Maybe I should just leave," he whispered. "We could talk tomorrow—"

Mrs. Arthur came out to the living room, wiping her wet hands on a dish towel. "Come in, come in!" she exclaimed warmly, as if the governor of Massachusetts had just arrived in her living room.

"Mom, this is Glenn."

"You're one of Robert's classmates? You go to Lovecraft Middle School?"

Glenn shrugged. "I guess."

"It's very nice to meet you. We'd love to have you stay for dinner. Does your mom know you're here? Do you want me to call her?"

"She lives in Arizona."

"Oh," Mrs. Arthur said. "How about your father?"

"You don't need to call anyone, Mrs. Arthur."

"Well, dinner will be ready at five. Let me fix you a snack in the meantime."

The boys carried bowls of pretzels and potato chips up to Robert's bedroom. Once the door was closed, Robert unzipped his backpack and the rats scampered out onto the carpet.

"This is Pip and Squeak. We'll need to swipe some food for them at dinner. Whatever you can drop in your lap without my mother noticing. They eat pretty much anything."

Glenn stared at the creature, fascinated. Pip and

Squeak seemed to relish the attention. They smiled, chattered their teeth, and purred.

"Which one controls the body?"

"I'm not sure. They might take turns."

"I thought Professor Goyle got rid of them."

"He tried," Robert said. "But last night I snuck into his classroom and took them back."

"You did not!"

"I sure did. And that's not the worst part."

Robert told Glenn the whole story. He started with Karina and the attic above the library. Then he explained how he and Karina hid in the supply closet and saw Goyle swallow the hamster. Then he described how he tried to return to the attic but couldn't find it.

"I've been dying to talk about this stuff all day. But who's going to believe we saw a giant squid come out of my locker? Who's going to believe any of it?"

Glenn chewed thoughtfully on a potato chip. "Nobody."

They sat across from each other on the floor, with Pip and Squeak between them gnawing on the corner of an old Monopoly game box. Robert didn't stop them; he was too caught up in the weirdness of the moment. Glenn Torkells, his least favorite person in the world, was sitting in his bedroom. Hanging out and munching on potato chips. Like they were old pals.

"And by the way," Robert continued, "when those tentacles grabbed you? I was pretty tempted to let them carry you away. Just so you know."

Glenn stared down at his lap, and his dirty blond hair fell over his face. "I know."

"That's all you're going to say?"

"What do you *want* me to say?"

"You've been a real jerk to me, Glenn. All the name-calling, the pushing, the shoving, the gummy worms. I used to wish that a giant monster would come out of nowhere and swallow you whole. I never thought it would actually happen."

Glenn didn't respond. He just sat there watching Pip and Squeak as they gnawed through the Monopoly box. Finally he reached into his pocket and pulled out a handful of wrinkled bills. "Here."

Robert counted the money. "Three bucks? That's your apology? Three lousy bucks?"

"It's dweeb tax," Glenn explained. "How much have I taken from you since I started? A hundred? Two hundred?"

"More like five hundred," Robert said.

"Then I'll pay back five hundred," Glenn said, wincing as he made the promise. "It'll probably take me a while. But I'll give you a little every week. I swear I'll pay you the whole five hundred bucks, all right?"

All Robert really wanted was for Glenn to say he was sorry, but he'd be happy to take the five hundred bucks instead. He supposed that, to a kid like Glenn, five hundred bucks probably meant the same thing.

"Apology accepted," he said.

"So what now?" Glenn asked. "What happens when we go to school tomorrow?"

Robert didn't know the answer to that question. Part of him wanted to find a trustworthy adult—probably Mr. Loomis—and describe everything he'd seen. But what he'd seen was impossible. In real life, tentacles didn't come wriggling out of school lockers. In real life, science teachers didn't eat the classroom pets. How could he expect anyone to believe him?

And what if Professor Goyle wasn't acting alone? What if other teachers at Lovecraft were just like him? What if Principal Slater ate hamsters every morning for breakfast? If Robert told the truth to the wrong person, he could end up in bigger trouble than he was now.

"We need to find Karina," he said. "She watched Goyle swallow that hamster and she didn't even flinch. I think she knows more about Lovecraft than she's letting on."

"So where do we look for her?" Glenn asked.

Before Robert could answer, he heard his mother calling. "Boys, come quick! You need to see this!"

Robert and Glenn hurried downstairs to the living room. Mrs. Arthur had the television tuned to the evening news. On the screen, a reporter was standing outside the main entrance of Lovecraft Middle School.

". . . live coverage with more disturbing developments at the new Lovecraft Middle School in Dunwich, Massachusetts. Just yesterday morning, we reported that seventh-grader Sylvia Price was missing, and her whereabouts are still unknown. This afternoon, we learned that Sylvia's twin sister, Sarah, has also disappeared. Two missing children in forty-eight hours. Should we expect more?"

The news anchor turned to the chief of the Dunwich Police Department, who gave all the usual warnings about avoiding strangers and staying out of unfamiliar automobiles.

Robert and Glenn exchanged uneasy glances. They both understood that they had narrowly escaped becoming the third and fourth missing students from Lovecraft Middle School.

And there would almost definitely be more.

CHAPTER THIRTEEN

The next morning, Robert was brushing his teeth when he heard a knock at the front door. He went downstairs and found Glenn standing on his porch.

"What's up?"

"Your house is on my way to school," Glenn shrugged. "I thought we could walk together."

"All right." Robert whistled for Pip and Squeak, zipped the rats inside his backpack, and pulled the front door closed. "Let's go."

It was a cool gray morning. It had thunderstormed the night before, and the potholes in the street were filled with rainwater.

"This is a nice block," Glenn observed.

"You think?" Robert had never heard anyone describe his street as nice. Most of his neighbors didn't even have grass.

"It's quiet," Glenn said.

Every few steps, the boys would pass an earthworm writhing on the sidewalk, washed up by the rainstorms, and every time, Glenn would reach down and fling the worm onto a muddy lawn. It seemed like weird behavior, but Robert didn't say anything. Lately, he was learning all kinds of weird things about Glenn Torkells.

"I've been thinking about what happened yesterday," Glenn said. "I figure the school must be haunted."

"By what? Giant squids?"

"Once I saw this movie about a haunted house," he explained. "It looked totally normal on the outside, but inside all this weird stuff kept happening. Stuffed animals floating around. The daughter got sucked into a television set. Finally they figured out the house was built on an old Native American burial ground. The spirits of all the dead bodies were trapped under the house, so they were rising up to haunt them."

"You think Lovecraft Middle School was built on an old graveyard?"

"It's possible, isn't it?"

Robert shrugged. "When you've got giant squids coming out of lockers, anything's possible."

They agreed to meet at lunch to research the theory, but Robert couldn't wait three hours to get started. His first class of the day was gym. He told his teacher he wasn't feeling well and asked permission to study in the school library. Once there, Robert asked Ms. Lavinia to point him to the old newspapers. It took him just a few minutes to find the September 7 issue of *The Dunwich Chronicle*, the local daily newspaper. There was a front-page article about the grand opening of Lovecraft Middle School. Robert scanned the text until he reached the important part:

> The new middle school is situated on five
> acres near the intersection of Grove Av-
> enue and Clive Hills Road. Longtime Dun-
> wich residents will recognize this land as
> the former site of the 120-year-old Clem-
> son Family Berry Farm. Angus Clemson
> deeded the land to the town of Dunwich
> upon his retirement five years ago.

It was enough to rule out Glenn's theory, Robert decided, and he nearly stopped reading. But then another paragraph near the bottom of the page caught his attention.

> Lovecraft Middle School is one of the
> most environmentally friendly schools in
> the United States and generates 90 per-
> cent of its own power from rooftop solar
> panels. The school was constructed al-
> most entirely from recycled materials;
> many of the doors, windows, floor tiles,

and masonry were reclaimed from the
old Tillinghast Mansion before it was demolished earlier this year.

The name sounded familiar. Hadn't his mother
mentioned the Tillinghast Mansion just the other
night? There was a pay phone near the entrance to the
library. Robert swiped his student ID card and then
dialed the number of the hospital where his mother
worked. When she finally reached the phone, she
sounded out of breath.

"Robert, what's wrong?"

"Nothing."

"Where are you?"

"At school."

"Why are you calling me?"

"I had a question."

She took a deep breath. "My goodness, Robert, I
thought you'd been kidnapped like those girls! Do you
know how much you've scared me?"

"I'm fine, Mom. Everything's fine. But do you

remember that story you told me the other night? About Crawford Tillinghast? Why did your friends think the house was haunted?"

There was a long pause. "I don't understand. You're calling me at work to ask about Crawford Tillinghast?"

"It's for a school project," Robert said.

"Can this wait until later?"

"It's important. I just want to know why you thought the house was haunted."

"Gosh, honey, I don't remember all the details. He was some kind of physicist, I think. He had a laboratory in his basement. There was a whole team of scientists helping him. And if you believe the rumors, he was summoning evil spirits. Inviting these ancient demons and monsters into his home. A lot of hocus-pocus mumbo jumbo, you know what I mean?"

"You said something about a house fire. When did that happen?"

"Oh, a long time ago. I was in middle school my-self. For thirty years after the fire, everyone in Dun-wich claimed the house was haunted. I have friends who swore they'd seen figures moving through the windows. Or heard strange chanting coming from inside. The cops used to drive out there every weekend to investigate something or other. I'm sure they were thrilled when the house was finally demolished."

Yeah, Robert thought, except the house wasn't *completely* demolished. Many of its raw materials were recycled into Lovecraft Middle School.

What if the evil forces were somehow recycled with them? Was that possible? What if all the hocus-pocus mumbo jumbo had carried over to the new building?

"Does that help with your project, Robert? Because we're short-handed and I really need to get back to work."

"Just one more question," Robert said. "You said Tillinghast was summoning monsters into his home. Do you know what they looked like?"

He glanced up and saw Ms. Lavinia watching him from across the library. She was holding a phone to her ear, but she seemed to be listening to Robert's conversation.

"Sweetie, let me be clear about something. Demons and monsters are not real. Crawford Tillinghast was a lunatic. And you're a lunatic for bothering me at work with this stuff, do you understand?"

Robert was tempted to explain himself but didn't

dare say anything with Ms. Lavinia nearby. He wondered if the librarian was friendly with Professor Goyle, if they ever chatted together in the faculty lounge.

He thanked his mother for her help and hung up.

CHAPTER

FOURTEEN

When the lunch bell rang, Robert skipped the cafeteria and went to the school computer center to do more research. Naturally Lovecraft Middle School had a first-rate facility with dozens of brand-new computers, printers, scanners, and tablets. The teacher, Mr. Padapolous, asked Robert to sign in using a digital touch screen.

Robert chose a computer in a far corner of the room, where no one could see what he was doing, and searched the Web for information on Crawford Tillinghast. He found a lot of weird articles in scientific journals. They had titles like "Ecology of the

Hyphalosaurus Species" and "Meditation: A Pinhole in the Time-Space Continuum?" and they were impossible to understand.

But eventually he found an article in a 1983 issue of *The Dunwich Gazette* with the headline:

EXPLOSION ROCKS TILLINGHAST
MANSION, EIGHTEEN PERISH

The article explained that the mansion had been built by Crawford Tillinghast's grandfather in the early twentieth century. The house was enormous and featured fifteen bedrooms, ten bathrooms, three kitchens, a ballroom, a piano room, and an observatory. Tillinghast employed three scientists and they lived in the mansion along with their families; at the bottom of the page was a group photo of everyone who lived in the mansion.

It was Robert's first look at Crawford Tillinghast. He was tall and thin and dressed in a white suit. Sitting in a large chair, surrounded by his employees and their spouses and their children, he looked like the grandfather of a large, happy family.

The article didn't describe the nature of their scientific experiments. It simply said that a machine in the basement laboratory had malfunctioned, causing a massive explosion that claimed the lives of all eighteen residents, including Tillinghast himself. Much of the building was spared, but the bodies of the employees were never recovered.

"There you are," Glenn said, dropping into the chair beside Robert. "I thought we were meeting in the library."

It was a funny thing: Just twenty-four hours ago, the sudden arrival of Glenn Torkells would have terrified Robert. Now, he was frustrated Glenn hadn't come sooner.

"I didn't like the way Ms. Lavinia was looking at me. I'm starting to wonder if she's part of it."

"Part of what?"

"All of it. Professor Goyle, the Price twins, Pip and Squeak. It's all connected, Glenn. Something really big is happening here."

Robert shared his findings from earlier that morning. He explained his new theory—that the haunts from Tillinghast Mansion had somehow been recycled, along with the doors and bricks and floor tiles, into the new Lovecraft Middle School.

"That's impossible," Glenn said.

"All of this stuff is impossible," Robert told him. "A tentacle pulling you inside a locker is impossible. But it happened, Glenn. We saw it."

His voice had become louder without his realizing it. Mr. Padapolous got up from his desk and walked over to the boys. Glenn tilted the computer monitor so the teacher couldn't see what they were doing.

Mr. Padapolous frowned. "These machines are for school use only," he said. "If you want to play video games, you can come back at three o'clock for Computer Club."

"We understand," Robert said. "We're just researching a little local history."

The teacher shuffled back to his desk. Robert wondered if Mr. Padapolous was friendly with Professor Goyle, if Mr. Padapolous was friendly with Ms. Lavinia.

Maybe Mr. Padapolous was part of it, too.

Glenn tapped the computer screen. "So what did you learn about this guy Tillinghast?"

Robert studied the photograph, studied Tillinghast's shock of white hair. "When I was spying on Goyle, he mentioned a Master. A person in charge of a plan. I'm starting to think Tillinghast is that Master. Somehow he survived and he's controlling all these strange forces."

Glenn studied the photograph, too. "The guy definitely *looks* like a grade-A weirdo. Though, in 1983, I guess a lot of people did. Who are all these other people?'

"Scientists. His employees. And their families. They all lived in the mansion together."

Glenn pointed to a girl on the edge of the portrait. She had short, dark brown hair that fell past her shoulders and a mouthful of metal braces. "This one's cute," he said. "The rest look like maniacs."

Robert took a closer look and blinked.

Glenn was pointing to Karina Ortiz.

CHAPTER
FIFTEEN

"What do you mean, that's Karina?"

Robert didn't know what he meant. But when he presented all the evidence to Glenn, it followed a certain pattern. Robert had never seen Karina in any classes. He had never seen her beyond the property of Lovecraft Middle School. And they had managed to squeeze into that tiny dark closet without bumping into each other.

Glenn was incredulous. "What are you saying? She's some kind of ghost?"

Robert tapped the photo on the screen. "I'm saying I know this girl. I've talked to her. And this photo is almost thirty years old. What other explanation is there?"

Glenn sat back in his chair. "This is just getting stranger and stranger. I'm starting to wish you'd just let those tentacles carry me away."

"We need to find her," Robert said. "We need to get back in that attic."

"I thought you already tried," Glenn said. "You told me you couldn't find it."

"That's true," Robert told him. "But I think I know someone who can." He glanced at the clock. There were just fifteen minutes until lunch ended, and then there was a mandatory school assembly to discuss the disappearance of the Price twins. Apparently a police officer was coming to give a lecture on stranger danger. "We better go now if we're going to make it."

The boys grabbed their backpacks and left the computer lab. Out in the hallway, two teachers were speaking in low whispers. They stopped talking as the boys approached. Their eyes seemed full of mistrust. One of the teachers brought out his cell phone and punched in a number.

"Don't panic," Glenn whispered, clapping Robert on the shoulder, like they were two old pals taking a friendly stroll. "Just keep moving."

From out of nowhere, Mr. Loomis shoved his way between them. "Glenn Torkells!" he exclaimed. "What did I tell you about hitting Robert?"

"Me?" Glenn asked. "What?"

"Last time, you got a warning. This time, it's a suspension. Come on, I'm taking you straight to the principal's office."

"Mr. Loomis, it's okay," Robert said. "Glenn and I are friends now."

Mr. Loomis looked exasperated. "Stop protecting him, Robert. If he doesn't get punished, he's never going to leave you alone."

"I'm not lying this time, I promise."

Mr. Loomis crossed his arms over his chest. "All right, fine. You're friends? Prove it."

Prove it? Robert didn't know how to prove it. What did Loomis want them to do? Shake hands? Hug?

Glenn cleared his throat. "Uh, I had dinner at

Robert's house last night? And his mother still cuts his spaghetti into little pieces. Like he's four years old. But I didn't make fun of him, because we're friends."

Robert thought this was a weird thing to say. Didn't everyone serve spaghetti cut into little pieces? Because it was easier to eat that way?

"Well, here's something you don't know about Glenn," Robert told Mr. Loomis. "On the way to school this morning, he decided to rescue ten thousand worms. He picks them off the sidewalk after rainstorms and moves them to the grass so they don't bake in the sun. I thought it was a little weird, but since we're friends now *I* didn't say anything."

Mr. Loomis looked from one boy to the other, astonished. "You really *are* friends, aren't you? How the heck did that happen?"

"Can we tell you later?" Robert asked. "We need to get to the library before the assembly starts."

"Fine," Mr. Loomis said, stepping aside. "I hope you find some good books. Have fun."

The boys hurried on their way.

When they arrived at the library, Ms. Lavinia was in her usual perch at the circulation desk. She saw the boys enter, picked up her telephone, and whispered a few words before hanging up.

Robert and Glenn had to walk past her to reach the fiction section.

"Can I help you find something?" she asked.

"Just looking," Robert said.

He turned down the nearest aisle, following it until they were out of Ms. Lavinia's line of sight.

"What now?" Glenn asked.

Robert knelt down and unzipped his backpack. Pip and Squeak scrambled out onto the floor. "Guys, we need your help. You have to take us to the attic. Can you do that?"

Pip and Squeak cringed. After escaping the attic via Robert's backpack, it was clear they didn't want to return.

"Please, guys," Robert said. "I know it's not safe there, but we're not safe here, either. We need to go back."

Pip and Squeak chattered at each other for a few moments, as if they were actually debating the decision. It seemed like Pip was willing to go, but Squeak needed some persuading. Finally they turned and set off down the aisle.

"Come on," Robert told Glenn. "They're going."

It was the same route he'd taken last time, through FICTION then MYSTERY then PARANORMAL. The shelves stretched upward as they advanced deeper and deeper into the maze. Books blurred past them. Pip and Squeak were running, and Glenn and Robert ran after them.

"Are you sure this is the right way?" Glenn asked.

"Definitely." The air was thick with the odor of moldy mothballs. "We're almost there."

After another minute or so, they arrived at a dead end. In the corner, barely visible, was the old wooden doorway that led to the attic. Pip and Squeak were standing at the base of it.

"Thanks, guys," Robert said, unzipping his backpack so they could climb inside. But Pip and Squeak shook their heads. They may have been willing to lead Robert to the attic, but they weren't going any further. "Fine," Robert said. "Wait here. We'll be back in five minutes."

Glenn hesitated. "You want me to wait with them?"

"Come on," Robert told him. Once again, he nearly stumbled walking through the doorway. He told Glenn to watch his step but it was too late; he tripped and fell to his knees.

"What just happened?" Glenn asked.

Robert thought he knew the answer, but he wasn't going to say anything. If Glenn knew the truth, there was a good chance he'd turn around and never come back.

They climbed the rickety stairs leading to the attic. When they reached the top, Robert pulled back the patchwork curtain and there was Karina, sitting at the round wooden table reading a book.

"What are you doing here?" She was even more surprised to see Glenn. "And why is *he* here?"

"We're looking for you."

Robert took a chair beside her. "I know your secret, Karina. It took me a while to figure it out, but I know." He reached out to touch her wrist, and his fingers passed right through it. "You died in the explosion, right? With your parents?"

"You shouldn't have come," Karina said.

"We need your help."

She shook her head sadly. "You've walked right into his trap."

"Whose trap?"

The patchwork curtain moved again, and Professor Goyle stepped out, blocking the exit.

"Thank you for coming, gentlemen. I believe you have something that belongs to me."

CHAPTER
SIXTEEN

"I knew you'd come eventually," Professor Goyle told Robert. He had forced the boys to sit at the round wooden table beside Karina. "You mentioned you'd been spending some time in my Master's house."

Robert shook his head. "I never said that."

"Of course you did! Don't you remember? When I caught you with the mutated rat, you said you'd found it in the attic above the library—but there is no attic above the school library! The only logical conclusion was that you'd found a way to cross over."

Glenn was bewildered by the entire conversation. "Cross over *where*?"

"This is the attic of Tillinghast Mansion," Karina explained. "I lived here in 1983. And I guess I still do. My parents were scientists who worked for Crawford Tillinghast." She looked to Goyle with disgust. "Until they learned the true nature of his research."

"Your parents were cowards!" Goyle said. "Master gave them an opportunity to change the world!"

Karina shouted back, "My parents wanted to help the human race, not destroy it!"

Goyle shrugged. "Well, it's water under the bridge. Their souls belong to Master now. So do yours," he told Robert and Glenn. "You boys won't be returning to Lovecraft Middle School, and neither will your little polycephalous friend. Give me the backpack."

Robert removed the bag from his shoulders and flung it across the room, knowing Goyle wouldn't find more than a few notebooks. The professor carefully searched each of the pockets.

"Now that's peculiar," he said. "I'm certain I smell rodent fur." He walked over to the patchwork curtain, sniffing the surrounding air. "Did your creatures insist on waiting outside? Were they afraid to cross over with you?"

Robert didn't say anything. He didn't want Goyle to know that he was exactly right, that he'd left Pip and Squeak at the bottom of the stairs, waiting in plain sight.

"Well, I suppose I should fetch them," Goyle said. "You boys sit tight. I won't be long."

As soon as Goyle passed through the curtain, Robert turned to Karina and whispered, "Don't worry. We'll give him two minutes and then we'll sneak out of here."

She didn't move. "It's no use."

"What do you mean? We can't stay here."

"Seriously," Glenn said, standing up. "I'm not waiting another second." He crossed the room, threw back the patchwork curtain, and nearly collided with a brick wall. "Where are the stairs?"

"He took them away. He can make them vanish and reappear," Karina said. "That's why you haven't seen me since Monday night. He's kept me trapped up here. Now we're all trapped."

Robert paced the length of the attic, searching for windows or ceiling hatches or *something*. He found an old flashlight and aimed its weak beam along the walls. Most of the space was given over to old books and bookshelves. But in one corner he spotted a pile of old blankets, a pillow, and a few small framed photographs. He realized he was looking at a young girl's bedroom. A very lonely bedroom.

Glenn drummed his fingertips on the table. "Look, Karina, I need you to start at the beginning and walk me through this. If we're inside Tillinghast Mansion, what happened to Lovecraft Middle School?"

"It's all around us," Karina explained. "Or rather, we're all around it. That was Tillinghast's plan. To create a parallel dimension where he could rule for eternity."

"Slow down," Glenn said. "You're already confusing me. I thought you died in an explosion."

Karina shook her head. "When the laboratory exploded, we didn't really die. We simply left your dimension and moved to a new one." She scowled. "My parents and I have been trapped here ever since, forced to help Tillinghast raise his army of monsters and demons. In this dimension, his house is never demolished. It's always 1983."

Glenn pressed his hands against the side of his head, like he was trying to keep his brain from exploding. "But in *my* dimension, his house *was* demolished," he said. "It was turned into Lovecraft Middle School."

Karina nodded. "Yeah. That's the confusing part. Somehow the transformation created holes between the dimensions. I call them gates. Places where you can pass from one world into another. They're all over the mansion and throughout the school."

Karina explained that the real Professor Goyle was a kindly old science teacher who had stumbled through a gate by accident. Now Goyle's soul was a prisoner of the mansion—and his physical body was being used as a disguise by Azaroth, an ancient demon under Tillinghast's control.

"An ancient demon?" Glenn asked. "Like an actual monster?"

"Exactly. Every time a person accidentally crosses over, their human soul is captured and one of Tillinghast's monsters goes back in their place. He's transforming the school one person at a time. And you guys are next in line."

"What are you saying?" Glenn asked. "Some monster's going to wear my body like a cheap rubber mask?"

Karina nodded. "Pretty much."

"And what happens to me?"

"Your soul will stay here. Trapped with Goyle's and the others for all eternity."

Robert knew that being trapped for all eternity wasn't the worst of it. Not by a long shot. The worst part was that, sometime today, a person who looked like him and sounded like him—but was definitely *not* him—would go to his house, talk to his mother, and sleep in his bedroom. There would be a monster under his own roof and his mother would have no idea.

Glenn pointed to the far end of the room, to the door barricaded with the wooden planks. "What if we rip off those boards?"

"You don't want to do that."

"Why not?"

"For starters, it goes the wrong way. Deeper into the mansion."

"Right, but you said there are more gates inside the mansion. What if we find one that brings us back to the school?"

"There are . . . *things* on the other side of that door. Things you do not want to meet."

"What kinds of things?"

Karina fell silent. She had just explained a number of very complicated concepts, but somehow the challenge of describing these creatures left her speechless. They were more horrific than words could convey.

"Things that fly?" Glenn asked. "Things that breathe fire?"

"How big are they?" Robert asked. "Six feet tall? Eight feet tall?"

Karina shook her head. She stared down at her hands, and when she spoke again, her voice was barely a whisper.

"They're spiders."

Robert laughed. "Did you say *spiders*?"

"It's not funny."

"Karina, don't take this personally, but you're a ghost. Spiders should be afraid of *you*!"

"There's a lot of them, Robert. Tillinghast knows I've got arachnophobia, so he keeps a bunch of them waiting behind that door."

"Then you just need to stand up to them," Robert told her. "The best way to face your fear is to deal with it head-on. Do you remember giving me that advice?"

"I do," Karina said, "but it was a lot easier to say it than to mean it."

The attic was quiet as they contemplated their choices. It was Glenn who finally broke the silence.

"We can wait here for Goyle, or we can stomp on a few creepy-crawlies." He placed his size-twelve boots on the table. "And I've got really big feet."

CHAPTER

SEVENTEEN

Glenn found an old hammer in the corner of the attic and quickly went to work. The nails squealed as he pried them from the wooden planks, as if to warn him he was making a terrible mistake. The first board clattered to the floor, then the second. Glenn was halfway finished with the third when he stopped to ask a question.

"These gates," he said, "what do they look like?"

"Picture a vortex floating in the air," Karina said. "Black water flushing down a black toilet. You just dive right in."

"What if the monsters follow us through?"

"Tillinghast has strict rules against that," Karina explained. "No one's allowed in your dimension unless they're properly disguised. Anyone revealing their true form is punished by death."

"We can talk more later," Robert said. "Let's get out of here before Azaroth returns."

Glenn wrenched the last board off the door.

"All right, everybody ready?"

Robert twisted the handle and pulled. The door opened inward with a loud squeal. Huge swaths of gray cobwebs clung to the back of the door. Robert aimed his flashlight into the darkness.

Ahead of them, a narrow stairwell descended into the darkness; it appeared to be cocooned in a tunnel of fine white silk. Robert placed his foot on the first step, testing the web.

"Is it sticky?" Glenn asked.

"No, it's fine," Robert said. "Come on."

They advanced single file: Robert first, then Karina, then Glenn. It was like walking on a staircase spun from cotton candy. Robert kept his hands at his sides to avoid touching the webbing. He was close enough to see strange white clumps tangled up in the silk. Some of these clumps twitched as he walked past.

"Egg sacs," Karina whispered. "Female spiders can lay up to three thousand eggs at a time."

Robert didn't see any of the grown-up spiders, but he wasn't trying hard to find them. There was no point in frightening Karina. He kept his flashlight trained on the steps, one at a time, all the way to the bottom.

They found themselves at the end of a long corridor. There were doors on either side, spaced every twenty feet or so, and light fixtures on the walls. It could have been a hallway in a fancy old hotel—except for the white spiderwebs spanning the length of the floor like a thin layer of fog.

Robert switched off the flashlight.

"Well, I guess that's the worst of it," Glenn said, brushing a few loose silk strands from his clothes. "That wasn't so bad."

"You're right," Karina said, taking a deep breath.

"I'm sorry I was being such a baby."

"Don't worry about it," Robert said. "Now how do we find one of these gates?"

"This is the fourth floor of Tillinghast Mansion," Karina explained. "These doors are all guest rooms and bathrooms. A gate could be waiting in any one of them. The problem is, so could anything else."

Glenn looked to Robert. "Do you want to go first, or should I?"

Robert reached for the nearest doorknob and turned it. Inside, the bedroom was draped in dust and more cobwebs. It had a large canopied bed, a chest of drawers, and a dressing table. He stepped inside and scanned the room, searching for signs of movement. "This one's empty," he announced. "All clear."

"Any gates?" Glenn asked.

"Nope."

Something dripped on the back of his neck. It reminded him of Glenn's half-chewed gummy worm from the first day of school. Robert reached up to wipe it away and found his fingers coated in a slimy green mucus.

"Uh, Robert?" Karina called from the hallway. "I think you should come out of there."

He turned to leave and more mucus dripped on his arm. He craned his neck, looking up at the ceiling—and the ceiling looked back. It was covered with a quivering green jelly that was spotted with dozens of eyeballs. The jelly began peeling away from the ceiling and Robert ran out the door, pulling it closed behind him.

"I'm not going to open any more of these," he said.

Glenn went to reopen the door, to see for himself, but Robert pushed him down the hall.

"Try the next one," he said. "We need to find the gate."

Glenn opened the next door. Robert didn't see what was inside this room. He just saw all the color drain from Glenn's face, and that was enough.

Glenn pulled the door closed. "I'm not gonna open any more, either," he whispered. "Let's just follow the hallway and see where it goes."

After another fifty feet, the hallway curved to the

left, revealing more closed doors and another long carpet of cobwebs.

And there, at the far end of the hallway, was a
swirling black vortex, just like the one that appeared
inside Robert's locker.

"That's it!" Karina said. "That's a gate!"

"Perfect," Glenn said. "Let's go."

But Robert noticed it had become increasingly
difficult to walk. As if his legs were growing heavier.
"Do you guys feel that?" he asked. Simply putting one
foot in front of another required a tremendous amount
of energy. "It's like gravity's pushing down on me."

Glenn tried to raise one foot off the ground. The
webbing clung tightly to the bottom of his boot; he
could barely lift it more than a few inches.

"That's not gravity," he said. "It's these cobwebs.
They're sticky here."

Glenn tried yanking the silk from his boot but it
just clung to his hand. It stretched from his boot to his
hand like pulled taffy. He was completely tangled in it.
"Help me get it off, all right?"

But Robert was stuck in a mess of his own. The webbing stuck to everything—clothing, skin, sneakers. The more he messed with it, the less he could move.

Karina was the only one not caught in the strands. She might as well have been walking on the beach. She glanced nervously behind them.

"Um, guys?"

Robert looked back. At the far end of the hallway a shadow was spreading across the walls and ceiling. Beneath it, lumbering down the center of the hallway, was a giant black figure. With six furious eyes, a spiked abdomen, and eight legs with bladed tips. It took Robert a moment to realize the thing was, in fact, a spider. And the shadows were thousands of baby spiderlings, following their mother toward dinner.

"What is that?" Glenn yelled.

"I warned you!" Karina said.

"You told us *scary* spiders. You never said *giant* spiders!"

"What's the difference?!?"

Robert glanced ahead to the gate. It was just five feet

away but it might as well have been a mile. He was stuck, hopelessly stuck. "Pull me out," he asked Karina.

"I can't." She reached for his wrists and her hands passed right through him. "I wish I could help you, Robert, but I can't."

Somehow Glenn was making more progress. He'd

managed to inch his way through the muck until he was even with Robert. Then he reached down and yanked Robert's foot from the goo, allowing him to take one halting step forward.

"Hurry up!" Karina called.

"Slow them down!" Robert shouted back.

"How do you expect me to slow them down? I can't touch them!"

"And they can't touch you, Karina. Remember that. Now do something!"

Glenn took another step toward the gate and dragged Robert along. By now they were surrounded by spiderlings, all over the walls and ceiling, thousands of them, in all different shapes and sizes. Some were as small as a nickel. Others were bigger than Robert's fist. All of them looked ready to leap off the walls and pounce on them.

Karina turned to face the mother spider. The creature stepped gingerly across her webbing, instinctively knowing which strands were safe to walk upon.

"Stay back!" Karina warned.

The mother spider bared her fangs and hissed. Karina screamed and the spider reared up on its hind legs like a horse, kicking with her forelimbs. Karina willed herself not to move, to let the legs swipe through her body. The spider seemed angered by its inability to harm her. It began to make a loud spitting noise.

"What are you doing?" Karina asked. "Why are you spitting?"

She realized too late that it was a signal. All at once, the spiderlings leapt from the ceilings and walls. There were hundreds of them, falling on Karina's face and hair, falling upon a girl who was and wasn't there. She closed her eyes and screamed until she heard Robert calling her name.

"We made it!" he shouted. "Come on, let's go!"

Karina opened her eyes and saw Robert and Glenn standing beside the gate. She began to run, and all three of them jumped into the vortex at the same time.

Suddenly Robert was falling, and when he landed he found himself face-to-face with a grinning skull. He was lying atop a life-size human skeleton. He screamed, flinging the bones away from him.

It took him a moment to realize he was no longer in Tillinghast Mansion. Somehow he had reemerged in Professor Goyle's classroom. So had Glenn and Karina. The gate had ejected them through the chalkboard at the front of the room; it was already disappearing, swirling away like water down the drain, leaving just a fine trace of white frost in its wake.

Glenn helped drag the skeleton away from Robert. "We did it!" he said. "We made it out."

"Did you see that spider?" Karina exclaimed. "Did you see how big it was?"

"You were incredible," Robert said. "That was the bravest thing I've ever seen. You totally saved our lives."

Someone applauded from the center of the classroom. "Yes, yes, congratulations." The three looked up and saw Azaroth seated at one of the student desks. "You managed to evade a swarm of baby invertebrates. But let's see how you fare against me."

He rose to his feet, and they could see there was now very little resemblance to the old Professor Goyle.

He was bigger, taller, more muscular. Two long horns protruded from his skull. His face looked bright red, as if his skin had been scorched to a crisp; his ears were long and pointy, like a bat's.

Robert ran for the door but it was already locked. He peered out into the hallway: Empty.

Where was everybody?

Then he remembered: the sixth-period assembly. Every student and teacher was in the first-floor auditorium, all the way on the other side of the building.

Azaroth walked along the windowsill, lowering and closing the blinds, so that no one could see what happened next. "I suppose you think it's easy being me," he said. "Trapped inside a suit of stinking human flesh. Eating your vile human food. Forced to lecture to stupid human children all day long. We all make sacrifices for the greater good. It's what Master requires. But sometimes I like to remove the camouflage and simply . . . breathe."

With this, Azaroth pulled off the rest of his disguise, shredding his jacket and tie with his sharp claws. Two large membranous wings sprouted up from his back, dripping with shiny mucus. "Behold my true form, children! This is how the Great Old Ones created me!"

"You're not allowed to do that!" Karina shouted. "If Tillinghast knew—"

"Silence!" Azaroth scratched his pointed claws against the chalkboard, creating a hideous sound that cut Robert to the bone. "No one can see us, child! The gate has been sealed!"

Robert looked to Glenn for help. But apparently this was all too much for him. Glenn was crouched down in the corner of the classroom, covering his head with his arms and mumbling to himself.

"Now, before I bring you to Master, I have something I want you to see," Azaroth said, stomping to the back of the classroom. A long red tail dragged between his legs, slamming against the student desks and chairs.

Azaroth ripped open one of the aquariums and yanked out Pip and Squeak by their tail. "I found your little friends, Robert! And Master is letting me keep them!"

He unfurled his glistening wings and they quivered with anticipation, spattering gooey mucus all over the classroom. Azaroth raised Pip and Squeak high above his head. The rats kicked their tiny legs in protest. Again Azaroth's jaw made a hideous snapping noise, and again it fell open like the mouth of a ventriloquist's dummy.

"No!" Robert shouted.

He lunged toward Azaroth but he was too small and too slow. The demon cracked his leathery tail like a whip and it struck Robert in the chest, knocking him to the floor. He landed in the corner where Glenn was still mumbling to himself. He sounded like he had lost his mind.

But then Robert realized that Glenn wasn't mumbling at all. He was *reciting*.

Kyaloh yog-sothoth f'ah!
Kyaloh yog-sothoth f'ah!
Kyaloh yog-sothoth f'ah!

It was the spell from the leather-bound book! But Glenn was reciting the words from memory, eyes squeezed shut, hands balled into fists, concentrating.

"Look out!" Karina shouted.

Robert turned just in time to see an enormous tentacle reaching across the room. It was followed by a second, then a third. They were coming from a gate that Glenn had opened in the chalkboard, and now they were tethering themselves around Azaroth's waist.

"What's happening? Release me!" he shouted. Pip and Squeak sprang from his grip and scurried into a corner. The demon grabbed at the tentacles but wasn't strong enough to wrest them loose. "In Master's name, I insist you let me go!"

Instead, more and more tentacles emerged from the gate, dozens of them. They snared Azaroth's arms, legs, and neck. Soon he was completely ensnared.

"This isn't fair!" Azaroth shouted. "I only removed the man flesh for a minute! Just one minute!"

The tentacles ignored his pleas. They retreated into the gate, dragging Azaroth along with them.

"Noooo!!" the demon bellowed.

The last things Robert saw were the horns on top

of his head, disappearing into the inky black vortex.

The gate lingered for just another moment. And then, like a giant eye blinking shut, it snapped closed and vanished.

Robert rushed over to Glenn and helped him to his feet. "Are you all right?" he asked.

"I'm fine," Glenn said. "Is he gone?"

"How the heck did you do that?"

Glenn looked up at him with a dazed expression. "Robert, I've told you a hundred times," he said. "I've got a real good memory."

CHAPTER
EIGHTEEN

The next afternoon, Robert, Glenn, and Karina met for lunch in the cafeteria. It was a beautiful day, and sunlight streamed through the windows.

All around them, hundreds of seventh- and eighth-graders were eating pizza and hot dogs and tater tots, oblivious to the bizarre world that was under their feet and just beyond their reach. The cafeteria hummed with laughter and chatter. It was just another Thursday afternoon at Lovecraft Middle School.

Glenn held a bag of gummy worms under Robert's nose. "You want some?"

"Sure." He took two and dropped them into his

backpack, where Pip and Squeak were already sharing a grilled cheese sandwich.

"There's something I've been meaning to ask you guys," Glenn said. "Why do you think Azaroth wanted Pip and Squeak so badly? I mean, why make such a big deal over a two-headed rat?"

"Because they're awesome," Robert said, reaching into the backpack and scratching his pets behind the ears. They still insisted on traveling with Robert everywhere he went; they accompanied him to school during the day and slept in his bedroom at night. Like bodyguards.

Glenn turned to Karina. "And what about the real Professor Goyle? Is he still trapped inside the mansion?"

"Yes."

"Can he ever come back?"

She shook her head. "Impossible. Unless someone defeats Crawford Tillinghast. Which is another way of saying it's impossible."

Robert wasn't so sure. Three weeks ago, he would have said that talking to ghosts was impossible.

Two-headed rats were impossible. Having Glenn Torkells as his new best friend was impossible.

If there was one thing Robert had learned in three weeks at Lovecraft Middle School, it's that *nothing* was impossible.

"Maybe someone just needs to stand up to him," Robert said, smiling at Karina. "How much do you know about this guy?"

"Man, listen to you!" Glenn exclaimed. "Yesterday we were nearly eaten alive by a million baby spiders and today you're talking about charging through a gate and fighting Tillinghast? Can't we just relax for a few weeks and do some normal school stuff for a change? Like classes and homework and detention?"

Robert grinned. "That's fine with me. For the next month we'll do nothing but regular schoolwork. No more gates, no more spying on teachers, no more getting lost in the library."

"And no more tentacles," Karina added.

"Thank you," Glenn said, and they all laughed.

In spite of everything that happened, Robert was

feeling good about himself. Sure, he'd never be like the characters in his favorite books, the kids with secret superpowers to help them escape any situation. But that was okay. He had started the school year with zero friends, and now he had three—or four, depending on how you counted Pip and Squeak.

Whatever weird things happened at Lovecraft Middle School, at least he wouldn't have to face them alone.

His thoughts were interrupted by the sound of a microphone humming to life. Principal Slater had climbed onto the stage at the far end of the cafeteria to address the students.

"Good afternoon, everyone," she said. "Can you please quiet down for a minute? I have some important announcements to make."

Principal Slater adjusted the microphone, cleared her throat, and continued. "First, I'm very sorry to announce that one of our faculty members, Professor Garfield Goyle, has taken an indefinite leave of absence. Professor Goyle has been teaching in Dunwich for nearly thirty years and he will be greatly missed. I'm sure many of you have questions, but at this point I do not have many answers. I found his letter of resignation on my desk this morning, so I'm still trying to understand the situation myself. I hope you'll join me in wishing Professor Goyle the best of luck."

There was a smattering of polite applause.

"Now for the good news," Principal Slater continued. "I'm thrilled to announce that Sarah and Sylvia Price returned home last night! The girls are completely safe, so you don't have to worry anymore. Please join me in welcoming them back to Lovecraft Middle School!"

Sarah and Sylvia climbed the steps to the stage, and everyone in the cafeteria applauded. The girls looked just like Robert remembered them. They smiled and waved to their classmates.

"Now I know everyone has questions, but I'm asking you to respect Sarah and Sylvia's privacy and let them talk when they're ready." She turned to the twins. "For now, girls, is there anything you'd like to say to your classmates?"

Sarah took the microphone and spoke in a flat, monotone voice. "It is nice to be back at Lovecraft Middle School. We must remember, classmates, that everything happens for a reason." She passed the microphone to her sister.

"That's exactly right," Sylvia agreed, in the same lifeless drone. "There are forces in this world we cannot comprehend. It is wrong to question the wisdom of the Great Old Ones."

Principal Slater nodded and smiled politely. "Well, yes," she said. "I'm not exactly sure what that means, but it's wonderful to have you back. Another big round of applause for Sarah and Sylvia Price!"

The cafeteria erupted with cheers. Sarah and Sylvia waved and smiled and then carried their lunch trays into the crowd. Plenty of kids moved out of their way, clearing a path, offering seats at their tables.

But Sarah and Sylvia ignored them. They weaved their way through the room, passing tables with girls and tables with boys and even tables that were completely empty. They seemed to be walking toward one table in particular.

"Oh, I don't believe it," Glenn muttered.

"Believe it," Karina grinned.

"So much for nice, normal school stuff," Robert sighed.

Finally, Sarah and Sylvia Price reached the table where Robert and his new friends were eating lunch.

Together, the sisters gestured to the empty chairs.

Then they asked:

"Are these seats taken?"

Turn the Page for a Sneak Preview of

THE SLITHER SISTERS

Tales from Lovecraft Middle School #2

BY CHARLES GILMAN

Slithering into bookstores in January 2013

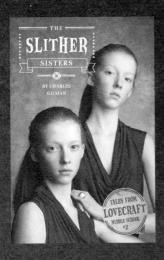

"This is the place," Karina announced.

Robert was confused. She had promised to bring him to a swimming pool. Instead she had led him to a door labeled "The Wilbur Whately Memorial Natatorium."

"What happened to the pool?" he asked.

"This *is* the pool," Karina explained. "A natatorium is a room with a pool inside it."

Glenn opened the door. "Holy cow."

Lovecraft Middle School had the biggest indoor swimming pool any of them had ever seen, fifty meters long and bathed in sunshine from skylights cut into the tall, arched ceiling. There were ten lanes for swimming, three platforms for diving, and a pair of empty lifeguard stands.

Robert, Glenn, and Karina were alone in the natatorium, but they wouldn't be for long. Sarah and Sylvia Price were due to arrive any moment.

"Where can we hide?" Robert asked, looking around. The air in the natatorium tickled the back of his throat. It was warm and humid and reeked of chlorine.

"Over here," Karina called.

Spanning the length of the pool were rows of metal bleachers for coaches, parents, and other spectators. Karina had already climbed behind the stands. It was a tight squeeze for Robert and even worse for Glenn; they had to crouch down on all fours to squeeze through.

"What if a teacher catches us?" Glenn asked.

"Don't worry," Karina said. "As long as we don't move, no one's going to see us."

It was true: To anyone looking at the bleachers, the kids were virtually invisible, camouflaged by the benches and rails and supports.

From their hiding place, Robert could see only the very surface of the water, as clear and still as glass.

"You're sure they're definitely coming?" Robert asked.

"They're here every day before lunch," Karina said. "The question is, why."

Robert wasn't sure he wanted to know the answer. The last time he tried spying on someone, he'd witnessed his science teacher, Professor Goyle, eating a live hamster.

Moments later, Sarah and Sylvia emerged from the locker room, dressed in simple one-piece swimsuits and chatting pleasantly. To anyone watching, they appeared to be perfectly ordinary sisters. But to anyone listening, they sounded like snorting, snarling lunatics.

"*Yh'nghai tsathogua dho-na*," said Sarah.

Sylvia smiled. "*Y'golonac chaugnar faugn.*"

"*Hgulet tcho-tcho, ep hgulut shaggai.*"

It was the same bizarre language that Professor Goyle had spoken—but what did it mean? Robert had no idea.

The sisters had reached the edge of the pool and were preparing to dive in when Sylvia stopped, scowled, and raised her hand. "*Gnai Glaacki!*"

Both girls glanced around the natatorium, as if suddenly realizing they weren't alone.

Together, they approached the bleachers.

A long forked tongue unfurled from Sarah's mouth, purple and black and eight inches long. It flickered this way and that, as if she were somehow testing the air. Robert remembered learning that snakes used their tongues to detect smell. He forced himself to remain absolutely still, hoping all the chlorine in the natatorium would mask his scent.

And it must have, because after a few moments Sarah retracted her tongue, satisfied they were alone.

"*Shai Shabblat?*" Sylvia asked.

"*Y'ai zhro,*" Sarah replied.

Together they raised their arms above their heads and then dove into the deep end. Robert watched the water lapping against the edges of the pool, the waves slowly ebbing until once again the surface was as clear and still as glass.

"What are they doing?" Glenn whispered.

"Shhh," Robert said.

He was counting off the seconds—forty-one, forty-two, forty-three—wondering how long Sarah and Sylvia could stay underwater before surfacing for air. Robert counted all the way to three hundred before stopping.

"How long can you hold your breath?" he asked Glenn.

"I don't know. A minute? Maybe two," Glenn answered. "They've been down there for five."

"They're not human," Karina reminded him. "Some reptiles can stay underwater for hours."

"Right," Robert said. "But why? What are they *doing* under the water?"

No one had the answer to that question.

"We need to see what they're up to," he said. "There

has to be a reason they come here every day."

Robert squeezed out from behind the bleachers and crept toward the pool. He wanted to glimpse the sisters without being seen—but they remained just out of view. He had no choice but to step right up to the edge of the water.

"Glenn? Karina?" he called. "You can come out."

His friends rushed to his side and looked down into the pool. Apart from several hundred thousand gallons of water, it was empty.

"What happened?" Glenn asked.

"They vanished," Robert said.

Karina shook her head. "They crossed over," she said. "This must be how they get back to Tillinghast. There must be a gate at the bottom."

Robert realized she was right. It would explain why Sarah and Sylvia returned to the pool every day: They were traveling back and forth between Lovecraft Middle School and Tillinghast Mansion.

He sat down at the edge of the pool, unlaced his sneakers, and pulled off his socks.

Glenn knelt beside him. "What are you doing?"

"What do you think?" Robert asked.

About the Author
Charles Gilman is an alias of Jason Rekulak, an editor who lives in Philadelphia with his wife and children. When he's not dreaming up new tales of Lovecraft Middle School, he's biking along the fetid banks of the Schuylkill River, in search of two-headed rats and other horrific beasts.

About the Illustrator
From an early age, Eugene Smith dreamed of drawing monsters, mayhem, and madness. Today, he is living the dream in Chicago, Illinois, where he resides with his wife, Mary, and their daughters Audrey and Vivienne.

Monstrous Thanks
Doogie Horner, John McGurk, Ron Fladwood, Jane Morley, Jason Heller, Jennifer Jackson, Mariah Fredericks, Steve Hockensmith, Jen Adams, Nicole De Jackmo, Eric Smith, David Borgenicht, Brett Cohen, Moneka Hewlett, Mary Ellen Wilson, Julie Scott, and Mary Flack.

LOVECRAFT MIDDLE SCHOOL

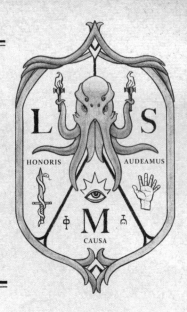

Is Now Enrolling Students Online!

- **GO** behind the scenes with author Charles Gilman!

- **READ** an interview with illustrator Eugene Smith!

- **DISCOVER** the secrets of the awesome "morphing" cover photograph!

- And much, much more!

ENROLL TODAY AT
LovecraftMiddleSchool.com